BETTER OFF DEAD

The footsteps receded at a run down the street. A moment later Dutch and Brannigan came pounding into the street from around back.

"Carl," Dutch said, "go get the harses. Ve use dem to pull dis harse off'n Longarm."

"Don't worry about me, Dutch. I can wait. See to the kid first."

"Longarm," Brannigan said gently, "the kid don't need anything now. He . . . shit, Longarm, Jimmy looks like his face was run through a sausage grinder. He's dead."

"Fug 'ou."

"Who said . . . "

"Oh, Jesus. He's still alive. C'mon, Dutch. Help me."

Longarm lay back, limp and thoroughly used up. If the kid was that bad maybe he wouldn't *want* to say alive. But that was for Jimmy the Kid to decide, not Custis Long.

While he lay there Longarm had plenty of time to work up a thoroughgoing measure of raw hate for Brad Dekins and Bob Dekins and whoever the fuck else they had with them. The bastards!

DON'T MISS THESE
ALL-ACTION WESTERN SERIES
FROM THE BERKLEY PUBLISHING GROUP

THE GUNSMITH by J. R. Roberts
Clint Adams was a legend among lawmen, outlaws, and ladies. They called him . . . the Gunsmith.

LONGARM by Tabor Evans
The popular long-running series about Deputy U.S. Marshal Long—his life, his loves, his fight for justice.

SLOCUM by Jake Logan
Today's longest-running action Western. John Slocum rides a deadly trail of hot blood and cold steel.

BUSHWHACKERS by B. J. Lanagan
An action-packed series by the creators of Longarm! The rousing adventures of the most brutal gang of cutthroats ever assembled—Quantrill's Raiders.

DIAMONDBACK by Guy Brewer
Dex Yancey is Diamondback, a Southern gentleman turned con man when his brother cheats him out of the family fortune. Ladies love him. Gamblers hate him. But nobody pulls one over on Dex . . .

WILDGUN by Jack Hanson
The blazing adventures of mountain man Will Barlow—from the creators of Longarm!

TEXAS TRACKER by Tom Calhoun
Meet J.T. Law: the most relentless—and dangerous—man-hunter in all Texas. Where sheriffs and posses fail, he's the best man to bring in the most vicious outlaws—for a price.

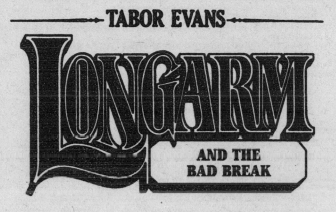

TABOR EVANS

LONGARM

AND THE BAD BREAK

J

JOVE BOOKS, NEW YORK

THE BERKLEY PUBLISHING GROUP
Published by the Penguin Group
Penguin Group (USA) Inc.
375 Hudson Street, New York, New York 10014, USA
Penguin Group (Canada), 90 Eglinton Avenue East, Suite 700, Toronto, Ontario M4P 2Y3, Canada
(a division of Pearson Penguin Canada Inc.)
Penguin Books Ltd., 80 Strand, London WC2R 0RL, England
Penguin Group Ireland, 25 St. Stephen's Green, Dublin 2, Ireland (a division of Penguin Books Ltd.)
Penguin Group (Australia), 250 Camberwell Road, Camberwell, Victoria 3124, Australia
(a division of Pearson Australia Group Pty. Ltd.)
Penguin Books India Pvt. Ltd., 11 Community Centre, Panchsheel Park, New Delhi—110 017, India
Penguin Group (NZ), Cnr. Airborne and Rosedale Roads, Albany, Auckland 1310, New Zealand
(a division of Pearson New Zealand Ltd.)
Penguin Books (South Africa) (Pty.) Ltd., 24 Sturdee Avenue, Rosebank, Johannesburg 2196,
South Africa

Penguin Books Ltd., Registered Offices: 80 Strand, London WC2R 0RL, England

This is a work of fiction. Names, characters, places, and incidents either are the product of the author's imagination or are used fictitiously, and any resemblance to actual persons, living or dead, business establishments, events, or locales is entirely coincidental.

LONGARM AND THE BAD BREAK

A Jove Book / published by arrangement with the author

PRINTING HISTORY
Jove edition / January 2006

ISBN: 0-515-14055-4

JOVE®
Jove Books are published by The Berkley Publishing Group,
a division of Penguin Group (USA) Inc.,
375 Hudson Street, New York, New York 10014.
JOVE is a registered trademark of Penguin Group (USA) Inc.
The "J" design is a trademark belonging to Penguin Group (USA) Inc.

PRINTED IN THE UNITED STATES OF AMERICA

10 9 8 7 6 5 4 3 2 1

Chapter 1

The new deputy was smart, handsome, young—God was
he ever young—and eager. Longarm wondered if he had
ever been that young. Or that eager. He doubted it. Damn
sure did not remember being like this kid. James Simpson
Wheelock III, deputy United States marshal. Behind his
back he was being called Jimmy the Kid. Longarm, and the
other deputies too for that matter, suspected some strings
had been pulled, strings of the political persuasion, to put a
badge onto Jimmy Wheelock's shirt.

Longarm had to give the boss credit though. If Jimmy
the Kid was foisted off onto Marshal William Vail by some
meddling politician, Billy never complained about it nor so
much as hinted that anything was unusual about the appointment. Billy took it like a man.

Billy Vail, on the other hand, was not required to ride
stirrup to stirrup with Jimmy Wheelock listening to the
kid's fabled exploits. To hear Jimmy the Kid tell it, he was
pure hell on wheels with a sixgun, could track lice on sandstone and had faced down at least half the most notorious
gunslingers west of the Mississippi. Yessir, Jimmy the Kid

1

was one hell of a deputy. It made Longarm purely wonder why Billy bothered to send him and Dutch and Carl Brannigan out of this deal. It surely would've been more efficient to just let the kid handle it by himself.

But orders were orders so Longarm and the other boys had to come along whether they were needed or not.

"Is this the place?" Jimmy the Kid asked as they reached the outskirts of Armpit, Kansas. And if it the town was not named Armpit then it sure as hell should have been because without a doubt it was the armpit of the state. Or the entire west. Or maybe the whole damn country. Arnpelt, Kansas, was . . . dreary was a charitable description.

It was, however, the place Billy's tipster said they would find the Dekins gang holed up. Brad Dekins and his little brother Bob, Harry Sanho and Earl Stanley possibly accompanied by a few others were expected to be here, resting up in the mineral baths and planning their next jobs.

The Dekins boys had been busy this past six months, taking down banks, trains and at least two post offices. They'd been recognized when they robbed the post office in Tensleep, Wyoming. Robbing a post office was a federal offense, and the crime was committed in a U.S. territory that fell under federal jurisdiction. That made the Dekins boys and their gang meat on the U.S. marshals' table.

Brad Dekins had sworn he would never be taken alive.

But deputy marshal Custis Long had heard that sort of bullshit a time or two before. Very rarely did that opinion hold when the man who'd voiced it was staring down the muzzle of a Colt .44. With luck it would mean no more this time than it had in the past.

"Yeah, kid, this is Arnpelt. Garden spot of . . . well, it would be a garden spot. If only it had water. An' grass. An' trees. An' shit like that."

"It doesn't look like much, does it," Jimmy the Kid said.

He sounded disappointed. Longarm didn't know what the hell he'd expected. Arnpelt was small, sun-warped, dry and butt ugly. Just like nearly every other small west Kansas town.

Longarm reined his horse to a halt at the edge of town and the others stopped beside him. Longarm was the senior deputy present and as such was in charge. More or less.

"There isn't a regular hotel," he said, "but if I remember correctly the saloon over yonder," he pointed to a two story frame structure on the south side of the road, "has rooms to let. That's prob'ly where we'll find our boys. The way I think we oughta do this, Dutch I want you t' take Carl with you. The two of you go around back of the place. Leave your horses and one o' you get at either corner so's you can cover anybody running out the back way or tryin' to slip out a window.

"Kid, I want you t' stay behind me an' on my left. Your job is to cover my back in case one of them tries to get in behind me. You hear what I'm telling you? I'll go in nice an' easy. You stay on the sidewalk and keep an eye on things. If anybody shows a fight, call out a warning and have at 'em."

"Why can't I go in first?" Jimmy the Kid complained. "I'm the best shot here. I should be the one to go in first."

On the way east from Denver, they'd had a few impromptu shooting matches. The kid won every one of them. Of course no one was shooting back at him and he took half a minute to breathe and fuss and get his sights set just so before he fired while Longarm and the other deputies just dragged iron and let rip. The kid even had the gall—or lack of experience really—to scoff at the others for hurrying their shots, the silly twit.

He would learn though. Give him time and he would learn. Starting, Longarm figured, this very afternoon.

"Watch yourselves now, boys," Longarm warned them all. "Dekins is a crafty son of a bitch. I don't know how comfortable he is here in Armpit but he likes to post guards and keep watch over things. He isn't as dumb as some of these assholes."

Dutch bit off a chew, worked it into the side of his cheek and spat. "Dey're all dumb or dey wouldn't do what it is dot dey do."

"There's dumb and then again there's dumb. There's also lucky. So keep your eyes open and don't take any chances." Longarm grinned at Dutch and added, "If the rest of us have t' haul you home draped over your saddle you'll stink something awful by the time we get you there. You wouldn't want to put us through that, would you?"

"Aw'right den. For you, dis vun time, I be careful."

"You're a gentleman an' a scholar, Dutch. Thank you. You fellas go on now. Me and the kid will give you three minutes to get around back. Then we come in at the front."

"Bueno," Brannigan said. Carl had a Mexican girlfriend, a hauntingly lovely girl whose English was almost nonexistent. He was trying with very little success to learn some Spanish so he could talk to her. Although with a filly who looked that good, Longarm didn't know why a man would want to waste time talking. He figured Carl was more than half lucky to have something like that for a playmate.

"I still think . . ." Jimmy Wheelock started in.

"Shut up, kid, an' do what you're told." Longarm reached inside his coat for a cigar—he'd gotten a box of panatelas in the mail just before they left Denver and was in the mood for one now—but kept his eyes on the windows of the saloon.

"Did you see something move inside that second floor window? The near one?"

4

"I didn't see anything," the kid said. "You've just got a case of nerves. You're jumpy."

Longarm grunted. "What I am is careful, kid. And still alive."

"Don't call me kid. I'm as good a man as you are. Or do you want me to call you grampap?"

"Well excuse me all the hell an' gone," Longarm snapped.

"They've had time enough to get around back," Wheelock said. "I'm going in." He bumped the sides of his fancy yellow horse and started down the street.

"Damn you, kid."

Wheelock ignored him.

Longarm had little choice. He could either sit there and let the idiot tenderfoot walk alone into a saloon that might well be full of hostile outlaws or he could follow. He damn sure was not going to race Jimmy the Kid for the saloon's batwing doors. Miserable little prick, he was thinking. Lordy, somebody tell him, please, that he hadn't ever, *ever* been that young himself.

When Wheelock was within twenty or thirty yards of the saloon the doors flew open and a girl came running out. She was dressed like a lady, not a whore, and she was screaming like there were wild Indians chasing after her.

"Help me! Oh, help. Help!"

She carried a beaded parasol and a matching handbag. She ran into the street practically under the nose of Jimmy Wheelock's horse. The horse shied and it took the kid a moment to get all four of its feet back on the ground.

The girl was pale and running for all she was worth. She dropped the handbag as she ran but made no attempt to turn back to pick it up.

She . . .

5

Longarm noticed something out of place. Something . . . it took him a moment to realize what was wrong.

Then he too screamed. At Jimmy Wheelock. "Get back, kid. Spur that hoss and go like hell."

If he heard, Wheelock ignored the order.

By then Longarm's blood had turned to ice. He wheeled his borrowed mount around and stabbed the spurs to it.

Because there was a thin stream of white smoke rising from the mouth of that handbag.

Chapter 2

Jimmy Wheelock and his pretty yellow horse absorbed nearly all of the explosion. Absorbed, too, most of the carpet tacks and small nails that had been packed around the explosive charge.

By the time the bomb went off Longarm was a dozen paces away and moving fast in the opposite direction. He was peppered with a few nails that penetrated his tweed coat and broke the skin on his left shoulder and lower back, but those injuries were not serious.

He could not say the same thing for his right leg however. When the bomb burst Longarm's horse leaped violently sideways. They discovered later that a good many tacks sprayed the horse's butt and belly, otherwise the cavalry-trained horse very likely would have stood firm despite the noise. The horse's feet slipped out from under it on the hardpacked earth of Arnpelt's main street, and it fell heavily on its side. Longarm's leg was caught beneath the animal. He heard the crisp snap of breaking bone and immediately wrenched the reins to haul the horse's head around so it could not rise. If there was anything he did not need it was to be caught dangling from a terrified runaway horse with his leg broken and boot caught in the stirrup. He had seen that happen to a fellow before and he damn sure did not want it happening to him.

Longarm heard the pounding of feet and a great deal of shouting.

Bad as his luck was about the leg, he was mighty lucky that his horse went down so that its body lay between him and the front of the saloon where the Dekins gang had holed up.

Now the bunch came boiling out of the batwings on the shoot. Shooting at him, damn them. Longarm could feel the horse flinch and jerk when the bullets slammed into it.

But better the horse than him.

Longarm already had his Colt in hand, but with his leg trapped underneath the now dying horse he could not raise up far enough to get a shot at any of the gang.

A shot? Hell, he never so much as got a *look* at any of them. He heard their voices. Heard their gunshots. Heard the ugly thud of hot lead striking soft flesh. But that was all.

The footsteps receded at a run down the street. A moment later Dutch and Brannigan came pounding into the street from around back. And a moment after that and a block away there was the sound of horses taking off at a dead run.

"That's them, boys. Go get the sons o' bitches."

"Aw, shit," Dutch said as he stuffed his revolver back into its holster.

"Get on them, dammit, afore they get away," Longarm snapped.

"We get on dem, Longarm. In da morning, you bet. Not now. Ve tie our harses two block over. Time ve get to dem, dat gang be too far to catchum before dark. Tomorrow we track dem."

8

"Yeah, okay. Sorry, Dutch. You know what you're doing as good as I do."

"Carl," Dutch said, "go get the harses. Ve use dem to pull dis harse off'n Longarm."

"Don't worry about me, Dutch. I can wait. See to the kid first."

"Longarm," Brannigan said gently, "there the kid don't need anything now. He . . . shit, Longarm, Jimmy looks like his face was run through a sausage grinder. He's dead."

"Fug 'ou."

"Who said. . . ."

"Oh, Jesus. He's still alive. C'mon, Dutch. Help me. Help . . . oh, God."

Longarm lay back, limp and thoroughly used up. If the kid was that bad maybe he wouldn't *want* to stay alive. But that was for Jimmy the Kid to decide, not Custis Long, not Dutch, not Carl Brannigan.

Longarm felt the horse's heavy body quiver once and a death rattle escaped from the animal's throat as it died. Longarm let go of the reins then. He no longer had to worry about the horse getting up and dragging him.

That would, though, have been easier to put up with than having to lie there and listen to the curses and moans while Dutch and Carl extracted what was left of Jimmy the Kid from under his dead horse.

While he lay there, Longarm had plenty of time to work up a thoroughgoing measure of raw hate for Brad Dekins and Bob Dekins and whoever the fuck else they had with them. The bastards!

Chapter 3

It was nearly full dark with lamps glowing through windows up and down the main street of Arnpelt before anyone got around to the task of lifting the dead horse away from Longarm's leg. A certain amount of scraping and dragging was inevitable, no matter how hard the men tried to avoid twisting and pulling the broken leg. He damn near ground his teeth to nubbins in order to keep from crying out aloud, and his clothes were dripping with cold, sour sweat. But in time they did get the sonuvabitch off him.

"Are you all right, mister?" a young local fellow asked, bending over Longarm and peering down at him.

"Shit yes, I'm just peachy." Longarm scowled at him. "How the fuck d'you think I feel, laying under that horse for the past couple hours."

"It hasn't been . . . oh, never mind. I guess it must'a seemed a long time, huh."

"Yeah. Plenty long."

"I'm sorry about that, but the doc was worried about your friend. We had to be extra careful with him."

"You did the right thing, son. Reckon I'm just a leetle bit cranky this evening what with one thing an' another."

"Yes, sir. Just lay right there. We got a cot coming. We'll get you onto that an' then carry you over to doc."

"I'm surprised you have a doctor in a town this small."

"Oh, he isn't a regular doc. He's our barber. Says he learned a bunch of medical stuff in barber college. And he's pretty good. He tends to pretty much everything around here. Haircut, shave, bullets removed or teeth pulled. Takes care of horses, hogs and milk cows too but he kinda draws the line at sewing up those longhorn range cows. He's got kicked by too many of them to mess with them any more."

"You're making me feel a helluva lot better about having him take care of me," Longarm said.

"That's nice," the young fellow responded, Longarm's sarcasm going over his head completely.

"D'you know how the deputy is?"

"The one that got all tore up, you mean? He was a deputy?"

"Deputy United States marshal," Longarm said. "Just like me." And if that was something of an exaggeration, well, Jimmy the Kid got it in the line of duty. Longarm figured he was entitled to some respect after that and never mind the details of it.

"I didn't know that. You're a marshal too?"

"All four of us. Out of the Denver District, U.S. Attorney's office."

"Those other two, the ones that weren't hurt, I saw some girl come and take them aside. I don't know what she said to them but as soon as she was done they hurried out and got their horses. They rode out at a dead run fifteen, maybe twenty minutes ago."

A tip about the Dekins bunch, Longarm guessed. One

of the floozies the gang was shacking with here in Arnpelt must have passed along some information about them. Maybe even where the gang was heading now.

Longarm hoped to hell the information was accurate. He would surely like for Dutch and Carl to bring the Dekins boys back to Denver in irons. Or just toss the sons of bitches heads into a bushel basket and bring that back.

"Here's Byron and Paul with the cot, mister. Marshal, I mean. They got it fixed like a stretcher, sort of. We'll put you onto it and carry you inside. Doc will get to you quick as he's done with the marshal that's dying."

Longarm clenched his teeth and steeled himself against the pain when this youngster and two burly farm boys loaded him onto an army cot and carried him to the barber shop two blocks away.

Chapter 4

"You shouldn't try to get up yet. You need bed rest. Several days of it at least. Maybe then you can get around with those crutches."

"I got to get going, doc. Dammit, man, you don't understand."

"I understand perfectly well, marshal. Those gang members have long since escaped. Those other marshals are trailing them now. All that remains for you to do is to go back to Denver. You won't be able to ride a horse for weeks, perhaps not for several months."

"I'm not staying here until. . . ."

"No, you misunderstand me. I wouldn't expect you to stay here all that time. But when you do leave you will have to be careful of your leg. It felt like it set properly. I'm not worried about that. But the splint I put on will only give you a certain amount of protection. Right now your leg is swollen. When the swelling goes down I can wrap and tie the splint again. Otherwise the splint could slip and the bones get out of alignment. If that happens," the barber shrugged, "you could be impaired for the rest of your life. Walk with a limp. Or not at all."

"How long before the swelling goes down?"

"I can't answer that, marshal. We will just have to wait and see."

"Can I send a telegram in the meantime? I need to notify my boss about what's happened."

"I'm sorry. We don't have a telegraph line. And the stage is scheduled only once a week. You've already missed the coach this week. It pulled out early this morning. It will be another full week before there is another so you might as well relax and give that leg time to start the healing process."

"What about a livery? Can I rent a rig here?"

The barber scratched the side of his nose for a moment, then nodded. "I suppose you could do that."

"Tomorrow," Longarm said. "Tomorrow morning first thing you can take the wrappings off my leg and re-tie them nice an' tight. Then I'll head back for Denver."

"I don't think that is a very good idea."

"All right. I'll make a note o' that. But I'm gonna do it even if I got to re-wrap my own damn leg."

"Marshal, have you considered that if you insist on driving yourself to Denver you will have to take care of a horse along the way. Feed and water, harness and hitch, everything. And if you put any weight on your leg when you are doing that, you could suffer permanent damage because of it."

"Thanks for your advice, doc, but I'm going whether you approve or not. If you want t' help, ask the livery man t' come by so's I can arrange for the hire of his rig."

The barber sighed. "You are a very stubborn man, sir, and not a particularly sensible one."

"Maybe not but I'm as charming as shit."

"Yes," the barber agreed. "Almost exactly that amount."

"You'll help me out, will you?"

"I suppose I must. I suspect if I don't help then you will take those crutches and go off on your own looking for Jay." Longarm assumed Jay would be the fellow who had a rig to rent. "I will bring him by after lunch. Will that do?"

"Yes. Thanks."

"Fine. Now lie down, please, and put that leg up. And leave it up. It will help reduce the swelling."

Longarm swiveled around on the side of the cot where they'd placed him last night. He lifted his bulky, heavily padded right leg onto the cot and lay down. Damn thing hurt like a sonuvabitch. He could feel every heartbeat in the throbbing pain of his broken and hugely swollen leg.

Fucking Dekins bunch. He hoped they gave Dutch and Carl an excuse to put them all underground. Every damn one of them.

Longarm closed his eyes and concentrated on conquering the pain.

Chapter 5

Deputy marshal Custis Long was a peeved and impatient man. But he was not a complete damned fool, and he had no desire to spend the rest of his life with a limp or a cane. Not if he could do anything to prevent it. He stayed in bed until the worst of the swelling in his leg subsided.

Finally though after two more days of grumbling and complaining, unable even to go outside because of the difficulty of negotiating the steep staircase on crutches, the Arnpelt barber removed the splint that secured Longarm's leg and felt it to make sure the bone was still straight and properly set. Then the doc put the slabs of padded wood back in place and wound layer after layer of linen bandage tightly around the shattered limb.

"That should hold for quite a while," the barber said, "but if you come across a real doctor between here and Denver I would suggest you have him look at it. I already told Jay you'd be leaving this morning. He already brought the buggy around. It's downstairs waiting for you."

"All right, doc. And I thank you. For everything."

"I'm just glad I could help."

Longarm said, "Don't you go an' be modest now nor shy when you fill out that voucher I gave you. The Ewe Ess government can afford to pay a good fee for all you done. And don't be forgetting meals an' supplies an' all that stuff. Time I get back I'll tell the marshal's clerk he can expect a big bill, so you go ahead an' charge whatever you think a big city hospital would want for all this care."

"Now that you've brought it up," the barber said, "I do have a question."

"Sure. Ask anything you like."

"It's about this voucher. Will that cover services for both you and the other deputy?"

"Yes, it will. Matter of fact, you should put on it whatever it cost t' bury Deputy Wheelock."

The doc gave Longarm a puzzled look. "You thought Jimmy died?"

"Well o' course. He was all tore up, they said."

"Yes, but the wounds were mostly superficial. I sewed his face back together the best I could and bandaged him. He is downstairs waiting for you. I, uh, I have to admit I was a little curious about why you never asked how he was doing. I hope you don't mind, but whenever he would inquire about you, marshal, I would make things up. Tell him you were concerned about him, asked after him, that sort of thing."

"Jesus, doc, I feel like an asshole. I thought the boy was dead sure enough."

"I think you will find that he is lively enough." For a moment Longarm thought the doc was going to say something more but he hesitated and then seemed to change his mind. All he said was, "If you are ready I'll help you down the stairs now."

Longarm was frankly shocked when he saw what awaited him at the foot of the stairs.

Jimmy Wheelock looked like something out of a picture book of old time Egyptian mummies. His right hand and arm were buried in linen bandages, and his head, neck and upper torso were likewise swathed in the coils of white linen. His right leg was bandaged also but not quite as heavily as the rest of him.

An opening was left over Wheelock's mouth, another where his nose would be and there was one more hole for his left eye. There was no opening for his right eye.

He was sitting upright on a chair, however, and had a cane in his good left hand.

"Jimmy, how the hell are you doing? It, uh, it's good to see you."

"How do you think I'd be doing? I won't be the same ever again."

"How bad is it, Jimmy?"

He held his right hand up. "You can't see it, but all that's under there are two fingers. And they're the useless ones. My thumb and pointer and middle finger are gone, completely blown off."

"Jesus!" Longarm blurted. "What about," he touched his own face, "what about your face? I, uh, I heard you got hurt pretty bad."

"I'll tell you what happened. I saw that girl run out of the hotel." The place was a saloon but Longarm was not inclined to pick any nits with the kid about it. "I saw her drop her purse. I thought . . . dammit, Long, I was going to help her. You were shouting something. I didn't hear

21

what it was. I stopped and leaned down to get her purse for her. That's when it blew up. I took the blast almost full on. My face . . . I don't know what I will look like now. I haven't had the nerve to look into a mirror, and the truth is that it may be a very long time before I do again. I don't have . . . I don't have a right eye any more, Long. It's gone. Doc said there was nothing left there. He says it won't be so bad. I can wear an eye patch. Hell, maybe I can wear a really big eye patch. Something big enough to cover my whole face. What do you think, Long? Will Marshal Vail want a deputy whose looks frighten small children and who doesn't have a hand to hold a revolver with? Are you going to do like everybody else, Long, and tell me how lucky I am to be alive? Well let me tell you something. I'd much rather that bomb killed me than to leave me like this. Much rather, goddammit." His voice was bitter and becoming increasingly shrill. "Are you going to tell me any of that simple-minded shit, Long? Are you?"

Longarm waited a moment, then said, "What I will tell you, kid, is that you fucked up. That's the simple truth of it. I shouted to you to get away from there. An' you heard me loud an' clear, don't tell me you didn't. You heard me but you wanted t' come to that pretty girl's rescue like some knight in shining armor. What you done was to fuck up. And, Jimmy, you are gonna be paying the price for that for the rest o' your life. I'm sorry it happened. Not as sorry as you but sorry enough. Fact is, though, that it did happen. Now you gotta live with it. Can you see a little? Walk? Feed yourself and all that shit?"

Jimmy's chin came up a little. Defiance, Longarm thought. And hoped although there was no way to see what expression might have been on the kid's face. Or whatever was left of it. "I can do whatever I got to do, damn it."

"All right. Then pick up that bedroll an' let's find the wagon that's gonna get us back to Denver."

Chapter 6

It was a buggy not a wagon, a rather nice little four-wheeled rig with shafts for a single, rather undersized roan pony. There was a folding top to shade them from sun or rain—but no side curtains for protection from really bad weather—and a single, handsomely padded seat to accommodate two passengers or three if they were really friendly. There was a luggage boot at the back of the rig where they put their bedrolls, saddles and a sack of supplies.

"We'll stay in hotels when we can find 'em," Longarm said, "or ask at farms can we bed there overnight. You can't always count on finding a place though so we're better off to be prepared in case we have to camp out." Longarm grinned. "That's a helluva thought, ain't it. A couple cripples like you and me camping out."

Jimmy just grunted. Apparently he had used up his allotment of words for the next little while. But he did help out, he being more mobile than Longarm with his crutches and broken leg while Longarm was the one with the better vision and use of his hands.

"Between us we make about three-fourths of a human

being," Longarm said as Jimmy fetched the hitching weight and dropped it onto the floor of the buggy, then crawled in. Longarm was already on the seat, driving lines in hand and crutches propped against the seat between himself and Jimmy the Kid.

It was mid-morning by the time they rolled out of Arnpelt, the day warm and the air pleasant. Except for having the broken leg Longarm was feeling pretty good, having had an unusual amount of rest forced upon him lately. He could not say that Jimmy Wheelock felt the same though. The kid moaned every time they hit a bad bump or dropped a wheel into a rut. He did not complain though. Longarm was a little surprised by that. He had kind of expected Jimmy to be a whiner.

The little roan, which was either a very small horse or a rather large pony, turned out to have a splendid road gait that was almost like the running walk that gave the Tennessee Walkers their name. It was swift and smooth and the roan acted like it could hold the gait hour after hour without becoming overly tired.

"Lots of hawks around here," Longarm observed at one point. "Lots of rabbits too. Which I suppose is why there's lots of hawks."

"Shut up," Jimmy snapped.

That ended Longarm's attempts at casual conversation. If the kid wanted to be grouchy then fuck him. Longarm was just trying to be pleasant.

They made, Longarm guessed, fifteen or sixteen miles before they came to another town, one with a hotel. By then it was late afternoon. There were still several hours of daylight remaining but it was unlikely they would find a better spot to stop for the night. Longarm pulled up outside the hotel without bothering to consult with Jimmy about it.

If the kid wanted to keep going he was welcome to do so. On foot.

"We need some help," Longarm told a boy who was squatted down beside an ugly white dog outside the hotel. "Tell somebody inside that we're out here, would you, son?"

"Yes, sir." The boy dashed inside, the dog going in with him. A minute later a young man came out to greet them.

"We'll be needing lodging and meals overnight," Longarm said, "for ourselves and this cayuse. And seeing as we're kinda banged up we could use help getting our things inside too. D'you have a downstairs room? Stairs are a mite hard to manage on these sticks."

"We'll take care of you, mister."

"Thanks. If it matters we'll be paying with a government voucher."

"That's fine." The hotel man gave them a looking over and added, "Seems to me you'd be the two deputies that got blown up over Arnpelt way t'other day."

"You heard about that, huh."

"Oh my, yes. The whole county has been talking about it. Most excitement we've seen around here since Ned Tyler fell down in his hog pen and got eaten alive by those sows. Y'know for the better part of a year you couldn't hardly give bacon away here, nor ham or sausage neither."

"Damn but it's good to know we've caused some entertainment," Longarm said.

"You can't blame folks for talking."

"No, an' I didn't mean to imply otherwise, friend," Longarm told him. As before, Jimmy the Kid said nothing.

Jimmy got down from the buggy and held Longarm's crutches while he very carefully lowered himself to the ground and got himself safely propped on his sticks.

27

"Go on in," the hotel keeper told them. "I'll bring your bedrolls in and take the rig over to the livery. Your room is down the hall, last door on the left. It isn't much but it's ground level, and I run a clean place. You ought to be comfortable enough there."

"I'm sure we will, friend. Thanks."

"My pleasure. You go on now and get comfortable. We'll take care of the paperwork and stuff later. You want me to let you know when supper is ready?"

"Yes, please."

Jimmy still was not feeling talkative but he did offer his one good hand to steady Longarm on the steps going up to the hotel porch.

Missing an eye, Longarm thought, and most of his right hand . . . that had to be a real bitch. Longarm couldn't blame the kid if he was in a bad mood over something like that.

"I hope to hell there's two beds in this room we got," Longarm said as he led the way inside, "but if there's only one then you best know it wouldn't be safe if you was to try and kiss me."

Longarm had not meant anything by that. He was just funning. Jimmy the Kid took the remark seriously although not the way Longarm might have thought.

"With a face like mine, Long, I don't expect I will be kissing anyone ever again."

Longarm shut his mouth and shuffled down the hall to the last room on the left just as fast as he could go.

Chapter 7

There was only the one bed but that was common enough. A man had to be prepared to share a bed when he depended on public accommodation. And at least this one was clean, with sheets that smelled of sunshine and, wonder of wonders, pillows that were soft and puffy.

"Not bad," Longarm declared. "Any preference which side o' the bed you get, kid?"

Jimmy did not answer so Longarm shrugged and dropped his hat onto the side of the bed nearer the door. There wasn't much room on the other side, not enough to allow easy use of his crutches.

Jimmy went around to his side of the bed and lay down. He lay unmoving, seeming to do nothing except stare at the ceiling. Up to him, Longarm figured. And the truth was that Longarm did not blame him for taking something like this hard. He'd been a good-looking kid. Now there was no telling what was underneath those bandages.

Longarm spent the idle time cleaning his revolver and polishing the inside of his holster with a dab of mustache wax. By the time the hotel man came to tell them supper was ready that was one almighty clean Colt and one slick-as-glass holster to keep it in.

Longarm stood and picked up his crutches. He used one of them to tap on the sole of Jimmy's boot. "Get up, kid. Time for grub."

The kid did not say anything. But he did get up and come along.

Supper was a cut above what Longarm expected. Beans, boiled potatoes and slabs of beef fried in tallow. It could have been worse.

They were halfway through the meal before Longarm noticed that the kid was eating the beans and breaking off some pieces of potato but ignoring his steak. It dawned on him then that with only one good hand Jimmy could not manage both a fork and a knife at the same time. He could not cut his meat. Without saying anything, Longarm reached over and cut the meat for him, then resumed his own meal.

The kid said nothing. But he did eat the steak.

"Are you old enough to drink, kid?" Longarm asked when they were done eating.

Jimmy's chin came up with what Longarm thought—hoped—was a small show of belligerence.

"Well I am," Longarm said, "and I'm wanting a snort about now. An' I'm hoping you will come with me." He grinned. "I'm not for sure how me an' these crutches are gonna get along after I've had a couple. You might have t' drag my sorry ass back an' pour me onto the bed."

Jimmy remained silent, but when Longarm got up and headed for the little saloon on the other side of the lobby he stayed at Longarm's side.

There were only two other patrons in the place. Wherever the locals went to do their drinking, this wasn't it. Longarm and Jimmy sat at one of the three tables. The other two patrons were standing at the bar chatting in low voices with the elderly bartender.

The bartender looked up and raised his voice. "What would you fellows be wanting?"

"Rye for me," Longarm said. Jimmy nodded. "Make it a bottle," Longarm amended. "An' two glasses. Four if those gents would care t' join us."

Jimmy's head snapped around with what Longarm suspected was annoyance although the expanse of linen bandaging gave nothing away as to his expression.

The whiskey was brought over by one of the patrons. The other fellow carried four glasses.

"Sit down, gentlemen, an' welcome," Longarm said. He pulled the cork and poured into all four glasses. The rye was a cheap brand, one he'd had often enough before.

Longarm introduced himself and Jimmy the Kid. The locals gave their names as Rance and Conrad. "Pleased t' make your acquaintance," Longarm assured them. Jimmy only reached for his glass and tossed the contents down the lowest gap in his bandages.

"You're those marshals, aren't you?" Rance said.

"We are indeed," Longarm agreed.

"The ones Bradley and his brother got the better of."

"Unfortunately," Longarm said, "I would have to admit to that as well. You sound like you know Dekins, sir."

"Oh, yes. They come through every once in a while."

"Been here lately?"

Rance chuckled. "Do you mean to ask did they come through after that little incident in Arnpelt? The answer is yes, indeed they did. They gave those other marshals the slip and stopped here to celebrate."

Longarm frowned. "Gave our people the slip, you say?"

"Oh my, yes. The boys were in very high spirits because of it, let me tell you. They thought it awfully funny."

"When was this?"

"They were here last night actually."

"Last . . . shit!"

Conrad laughed. "You thought they would be miles and miles away by now, didn't you? Just like those other deputies did. Oh, the Dekins boys are too smart for you, that is the truth of it. They claim there isn't a marshal alive who can keep up with them."

"Mister, so far I don't have anything to show that would say different," Longarm told him.

"Exactly," Rance said.

"I don't suppose they said where they was going next?" Longarm asked.

"No, they didn't say that."

"Any idea where they might've gone though?"

Rance shook his head. Conrad said, "Not me. Sorry."

"Just thought I'd ask," Longarm said. "Not that I'd know how to tell my friends if I did find out. Sure wish I could pull them back though if they're off on a wild goose chase."

"Chasing will-o'-the-wisps is more like it. Bradley and Bob are like that. They leave false trails then just disappear only to pop up again where you least expect them."

"Uh huh." Longarm finished his drink but was no longer in much of a mood for socializing. He motioned for Jimmy to come with him and left the rest of that bottle for Rance and Conrad to enjoy.

The remainder of that evening and night was spent in silence on his part as well as Jimmy's.

Chapter 8

"I have something to tell you."

"In a minute, there's something I want to say to you first."

"You go first."

"No, you."

Jimmy the Kid broke his silence at the breakfast table just as Longarm opened his mouth to speak. The kid clammed up again after that first abortive attempt to say what was on his mind.

Longarm got stubborn about it too then and decided the kid could go to hell if he pleased but if he wanted to say something he was just going to have to spit it out. Longarm went back to his sausage and eggs. The kid was having oatmeal, which needed no cutting and could easily be handled with just a spoon. Even that seemed a little awkward for him; he just was not accustomed to using his left hand. Yet.

"All right," Jimmy said finally, dropping his spoon into his empty bowl. "What I want to tell you is this. I won't be going back to Denver with you."

Longarm stiffened. "You aren't gonna do something stupid, are you? Like . . . you know."

"Like kill myself?"

Longarm let silence answer that.

"No. No, that isn't what I have in mind. I won't say I haven't thought about it. But . . . not yet, I won't. There is something I have to do first. Then I can think about whether I want to go on living looking like I do now."

"Something that's keeping you from going back to Denver now?"

Jimmy nodded.

"Funny thing," Longarm said, "but what I was wantin' to tell you is that I ain't heading back right now either."

"Why not?"

"You heard what those jaspers was saying last night. The Dekins boys an' their gang have sent Dutch and Brannigan on a wild goose chase while they slide off in another direction. You heard them say that."

"That's right," Jimmy agreed.

"Well, dammit, I ain't gonna let them get away with blowing us up. I come out here to bust that gang up and arrest the bunch of them." He cleared his throat and scowled. "I still aim to do that."

"That's what you wanted to tell me, that you are going to head after the Dekins gang instead of going back to check in with Marshal Vail?"

"That's right, boy. I figure they're bound t' have a stagecoach run through here. You can take the coach an' . . ."

"Whoa," Jimmy said, holding his one good hand up palm outward. "The thing I've been trying to say to you is that I don't intend to go back either because . . . well, because I intend to go after the Dekins gang too."

"You? You're all blowed up, boy."

"Have you looked at yourself, Long? You're on crutches. At least I can move freely."

"You only got one hand to work with."

"How many hands does it take to shoot a pistol?"

"You ever do any shooting left-handed?" Longarm countered.

"I intend to. And I think once these bandages are off I can learn to shoot a rifle or a shotgun well enough too. I still have two fingers left on this hand, you know."

"You're crazy. You know that, don't you?"

"No crazier than you, Long, thinking you can go chasing after a gang of murderers when you are on crutches. How fast can you get a gun out when your hands are occupied with crutches?"

"All right, dammit, we're agreed that we're both crazy. Be that as it may, kid, I figure t' go after them."

"So do I."

"You'd ought to go to Denver. Heal up some before you do something like this."

"So should you. And my name is James. Not 'kid'. You can call me Jimmy if you like, but I do not like being called Jimmy the Kid."

"You know 'bout that, huh."

Jimmy didn't answer.

"All right. I reckon you're entitled. An' while we're on the subject, Jimmy. You can call me Longarm. It's what the rest o' the guys all do."

Jimmy nodded. Longarm got the impression he was about to say something. But he did not. After a few moments he said, "How do we go about this?"

Longarm grinned. "First thing, ki . . . Jimmy, we make a stop to the hardware store I seen down the street. We're gonna buy you a good scattergun an' a shitpot full o' pistol cartridges so's you can get in some practice shooting that Colt of yours left-handed. After that, we take out after the sons o' bitches. Wherever they've went we'll be right behind them. We'll stop whenever Brad and Bob Dekins are dead or in custody. Not a minute sooner."

"All right, damn it," Jimmy said. "All right."

"Now help me get up, will you? My damn crutches have fallen."

Jimmy began to laugh. "You and I make one hell of a pair, Long. I mean, Longarm. What was it you said yesterday? Between the two of us we make about three-quarters of a whole human being?"

"Did I say that? What I meant t' say, kid . . . James . . . is that between the two of us we make one hellacious fine fighting machine. Now are you gonna just set there on your skinny, ass or are you gonna hand me those crutches like I asked you to?"

Jimmy sat there a moment longer, still laughing. Then he sobered and stood to collect Longarm's sticks and hand them to him. "Up and at them, deputy. Let's go catch us some bad guys."

Chapter 9

"Where are you going?"

"To catch the Dekins gang, o' course."

"But the hardware store is over there. I thought you said . . ."

"Trust me, James m' lad. We have a stop to make before we load up with stuff that needs carrying. Come to think of it, we need t' make two stops first. The second will be at the livery to get the buggy. There's no sense dragging all that heavy ammunition an' shit by hand when we can load it into the rig an' drive it instead."

"All right, that's the second stop. So what is the first?"

Longarm just laughed. And winked at him.

They hobbled down to the edge of town—it wasn't all that far for the town, such as it was, was even smaller than Arnpelt—to a low-roofed, tumbledown, half-sod shanty.

"What is this place?" Jimmy asked when it became apparent that this ugly little building was their destination.

"This, m' boy, is a slop chute. Hog ranch. Saloon for the working stiff. It's a shame you don't recognize it too. Means your education has been lacking."

37

"I know about saloons," Jimmy retorted.

"Good for you. Now hush up an' pay attention."

They entered, Longarm on his crutches the first to pass through the few strands of fly beads that did nothing to protect the doorway, Jimmy the Kid close limping only slightly close behind him.

There were three patrons in the place at that early hour. Or two, depending on whether one wanted to count the drunk who was passed out in his own puke in a corner.

The interior of the saloon was dark and smelled of urine and stale beer. The floor was dirt; no one bothered to spread sawdust on it.

"Walk around the muddy spots," Longarm suggested. "You don't know what's caused them."

Longarm led the way to the rough plank bar where the bartender greeted them with a scowl. "Hospital burn down and put your invalids out on the street, did it?"

"Something like that. Funny thing about fires, though. They make me horny. Where's your whores?"

"Where any sensible whore is at this time of the damn morning, mister. They're sleeping. Or passed out. One or the other."

"Then wake two of them up. Me and my friend are fixing to leave town an' we want to get our ashes hauled before we leave all these bright city lights behind us."

"It's nine o'clock in the damn morning, mister. I can't wake them this early. They'd bite my damn head off."

Longarm pulled a ten dollar gold eagle out of his pocket and laid it on the bar. "So don't wake them up. Just roll 'em on their backs and pull their legs apart."

"You don't want no change from that? They aren't but twenty-five cent whores."

"I told you, we're horny. How many of them d'you have back there?"

"Two," the barman said.

"See?" Longarm said cheerfully. "Just enough."

"I'll go shake the girls out. You want a beer while you wait?"

Longarm shook his head. The bartender disappeared toward the back of the establishment. The two early morning drinkers finished their beers—the start of a new day of drinking or the end of a very long one, Longarm could not tell which—and left, leaving the unconscious drunk in the corner as the only other customer.

Jimmy leaned close to Longarm and whispered. "What in the hell are we doing here?"

"We are lookin' for information, son. Do you happen t' know where the Dekins bunch was heading when they rode outa here?"

"No, of course not," Jimmy said.

"Well one o' these girls just might. Take a lesson in law enforcement, James. D'you want information about a bad boy, go an' ask a bad girl. Whores can be your best possible source of information."

"That makes sense. But what about . . . you know."

"Kid, after you've paid for a service there's no harm in enjoying it, even if it is in the line o' duty. If you feel a yen to fuck the girl, go head. Jump right on. Or she'll suck your dick if you'd rather that. God knows they been paid well enough."

"Su . . . they really do that? In the mouth, I mean?"

"My God, Jimmy, don't tell me you've never been sucked."

"Of course not. I wouldn't . . . I mean . . ."

"Oh my, d'you ever have a treat comin'. And I mean that in several different ways. This girl you'll be with this morning. Tell her t' blow you. No, I insist on it. It's different. Mighty nice. You're gonna love it."

"But what about what I look like? No girl will want to be with me."

"Jimmy, these girls is whores. They'd fuck a bull buffalo if they was paid enough. And anyway, no one can see your face. Hell, I got no idea how bad you was chopped up back there. All I can see is bandages. That's all they'll see too. Ain't nothing scary about seeing a bandage."

"I . . . maybe I should keep that in mind."

"Maybe you should," Longarm agreed. "But mind what I told you. Have your fun. Get your gun off in that old gal's mouth. But while you're enjoying yourself in there, ask her some questions: You don't hafta be coy about it nor try an' trick her. She'll already know that we're deputies, so go right ahead an' ask what we want t' know. An' to make sure she isn't soft on one of the gang an' sends us off on a wild chase like Dutch and Carl are, tell her there's a reward that she could get if the stuff she tells us leads t' those boys being caught."

"Is there really a reward?" Jimmy asked.

"Yes, there is," Longarm said solemnly. He had no idea if there was or not.

"And . . . I mean . . . she would really put it in her mouth?"

"Jimmy m' lad, you are gonna love this," Longarm said, pointing toward the back door where the bartender had reappeared and was beckoning for them to follow.

Chapter 10

The girls were about what might have been expected. Both of them were dumb, dumpy little farm girls with bad teeth and pasty complexions. Since the kid was so damn innocent Longarm let him take his pick between them.

Jimmy chose a plump little giggler with blue eyes and a button nose. She looked to be no more than sixteen or seventeen. That left Longarm with a dark-haired girl who looked like she was in her early thirties or thereabouts. She had a vacant expression and hair that looked like it hadn't been washed since she quit sucking her mother's tit.

Longarm had that thought and then smiled. He hooked a finger under the chin of Jimmy's girl and tipped her face up. "Do him French style, honey. He's never had that an' he might be too shy to ask, but you do him good, you hear?"

The blue eyes went wide and she commenced to grin and to giggle. Her expression almost made her pretty. Almost. "Sweetie, do you mean you never? Honest and for real? Well darlin', I am going to do you so sweet and nice you won't never forget Annie Mae. Now you just come along with me, sweetheart, and we will have us some real special fun, you hear?"

The girl hugged Jimmy's arm and took him by the hand to lead him into a room. Longarm made note of which room Jimmy was in—just in case there was the sort of trouble that he might need to know—then turned to the other girl.

"What's your name?"

She hesitated for a moment. He got the idea that she was trying to remember . . . and finding the task difficult. "June," she finally came up with. He felt like complimenting her for being able to figure it out. "In here," she said.

She led the way into a tiny, dark room that held a cot, a packing crate that had a very small lamp sitting on it and an unframed engraving of the Virgin Mary tacked on the wall over the bed. The picture seemed grossly out of place. The cot had a blanket on it but no sheet and no pillow.

June was wearing a loose wrapper and nothing else. She untied the strip of cloth that held it closed and let it fall off her shoulders. She kicked the garment into a corner and lay down with her legs spread and eyes closed. The color of her flesh reminded him of suet. Her tits were wrinkled and floppy, the nipples positively huge. About half the tit was nipple. Longarm looked at her and rejoiced in the fact that he was not required to actually fuck her.

"You can put your robe back on," he said.

"You want me to get dressed?"

"That's right."

"No."

"Why not?"

"I don't want you dribbling your jism all over my wrapper, mister."

The wrapper was lying on the floor and hadn't looked all that clean to begin with but now she was worried about

42

soiling it? "Besides, I don't go in for any of that weird stuff. You know? If you wanta fuck that's fine, but I won't suck you and I won't take it in the ass and you can't fuck me between my tits. Now if you want to fuck that's fine. If you don't that's fine too."

"I want to talk," Longarm said.

"Jesus God, mister, you want me to tell you how come I'm a whore? Or do you want me to tell you how big your cock is and how it's the best I ever had and how you drive me crazy with it? Is that what you want, mister?" She rolled her eyes and recited from memory, "Just lucky, I guess. Yours is the biggest I ever seen." Longarm's fly was still buttoned and he damn sure intended to keep it that way. "Baby baby, you're the best. You drive me plumb crazy." The words came out in a dull monotone. "Baby, I love you."

"Sure you do," Longarm said. He pushed her legs to the side—she really needed to wash her feet; the soles were filthy—and rather gingerly sat on the foot of the bunk, splinted leg extended and crutches held in one hand. "I'm a deputy United States marshal. Did you already know that?"

She shrugged, which could have been taken as a yes or a no, whichever way he wanted.

"I'm looking for the Dekins gang. Bradley and Bob and their boys were here just a day or two back. D'you remember them?"

Another shrug.

"There is a reward for their capture. If you help me find them you could collect that reward money." He paused for a second and added, "It's five hundred dollars." That sounded like a pretty believable amount, he thought, and ought to seem a fortune to a two-bit whore in a little dipshit town in Kansas. "That money could be yours."

The girl sat up on the bed, her tits sagging to her waist.

She looked at him, genuinely looked at him for the first time. Her expression remained dull and uninterested however.

"Mister, the men come in here; I lay down and they fuck me. I don't see their faces. I don't know their damn names. I don't give a shit who or what they are. And they can talk all they want but I never listen to any of their shit. Never. Now if you want to fuck, that's fine. You bought me. You're entitled. But I don't know nothing about some gang and I don't care neither." She lay back down again and opened her legs, ready to accept his pecker if he wanted to use it but supremely indifferent to anything Custis Long might want or say or do.

Longarm did not know if June was telling the truth or not. But he was reasonably sure he was not going to find out either way. He hoped Jimmy the Kid was doing better with Annie Mae.

Chapter 11

"Damn, Longarm, that was wonderful." Jimmy was bubbling over with enthusiasm. Longarm could not remember back far enough to a time when he would have been that excited over a simple blow job. It was a reminder of just how damned young the kid was. It was pleasing though to see that Jimmy was finally taking an interest in something other than his own misfortune.

"Liked that, did you?" Longarm said over the rim of the beer he'd been sipping at while he waited for Jimmy to get done.

"Yes, I did, and it won't be for the last time either. I know that for a fact. Something else I know is that I'm not going to forget about these bandages. They really do keep someone from seeing what is under them. They might guess, but they won't really know. As long as I wear them I can go out in public."

"That's fine. Hey, watch it. You like to kicked my crutch. If you make me fall down an' break this other leg, you're gonna have to carry me everyplace."

"Oh! Sorry."

45

"Jeez, Jimmy, I'm just funning you. An' I'm glad you had such a nice time with your girlie. But I sure as hell hope she had more t' say than mine did. I couldn't get shit outa that one."

"Just leave it to me, old timer," Jimmy said. Longarm could tell from his tone of voice that he was grinning under those wrappings. The kid really was in good humor thanks to little Annie Mae.

"Old timer?"

"Well . . . you know."

"I know I just might take a notion t' take you over my knee an' spank your scrawny ass. What did the girl say?"

"She said she was with a couple of the Dekins boys. Not the brothers themselves but two of their gang. She said they told her they were headed to Fort Larned. Something about needing to meet a man there, a sergeant. Does that make any sense?"

"Not to me, it don't, but then I'm not one of the Dekins brothers."

"She says they were supposed to wait around up here a while longer before they were scheduled to meet up with this sergeant, but we came along and spoiled that plan."

"Did she know anything about who or why or when this meeting is supposed t' take place? Or what for?"

"If the guys she was with knew they didn't tell her about it. She thinks probably they didn't know or they likely would have said. She said . . . she said they were both with her at the same time. Imagine that. Two guys at once. She said she can take three if she has to but that's kind of uncomfortable."

"Yeah, I can see how it might be."

"Imagine that," Jimmy said again.

Longarm got the distinct impression that Jimmy the Kid hadn't had a whole hell of a lot of experience when it came to women and most especially with the sort of women that a man could actually fuck. Probably most of the women—girls—Jimmy knew in the past were girls who sat in the parlor all prim and prissy and wanted to play the piano and sing hymns. There was a place for that too of course but Longarm preferred the kind of woman who sweats and farts and likes to make the beast with two backs.

"Larned, huh?" Longarm said, getting back to the subject at hand.

"Do you know it?"

"Of course. Larned is one o' the forts built to protect the Santa Fe Trail from Injuns and other raiders. It's on the Arkansas, downriver a piece from Fort Dodge. From here it's," Longarm paused to think, "I'd say from here it's maybe eighty or a hundred miles. More east than south."

"Annie Mae didn't know where the gang will go to finish waiting until it's time for them to meet that sergeant."

"But they still have to wait for a spell?"

"That's what she said, yes."

"Then we just might have time to get there ahead of them. What do you think?"

"I'm game."

"Good." Longarm peered into his mug for a moment. The beer had been in the keg too long and was flat and bitter. He set the mug down and left the rest of it. "Then get your shotgun and let's go."

"Whoa."

"What are we stopping for?"

Longarm pointed to the grove of trees on the bank of a small creek just off the public road. "This looks like a good-enough spot."

"Good enough for what?"

47

"Good enough for you learning how t' shoot."

"I know how . . . oh. You mean with half a hand."

"Yeah. So to speak I reckon I do. But you can learn to shoot your pistol left-handed. The shotgun too."

Jimmy hopped down from the buggy, gathered Longarm's crutches and helped him down too, then he broke into the case of .44-40 ammunition they'd purchased and got one box of fifty rounds out of it.

"There's a sharp drop over on the other side o' the creek. You can shoot into that without murdering some farmer's milk cows."

"I can't reach my revolver, Longarm."

"Not on your right side where you always carried it before. Pull your gunbelt around so the holster hangs on your left. Yeah, that's better. The butt is pointing the wrong way now, so when you wanta get at the thing, twist your wrist around an' draw that way."

"It's awkward."

"O' course it is. Anything is at first. But you can get used to it in time. Won't be as fast to get out maybe, but in a fight the winner isn't the guy who makes the quickest noise, it's the fella that makes the actual first hit. That ain't a bad thing t' remember. Now let's see how you do shooting at a mark with that hand. Don't think about bein' fast. Just think about trying to hit what you're aiming at."

Jimmy raised his pistol, cocked it and said, "I'm aiming at that clump of roots sticking out of the bank. Do you see it?"

"Ayuh. Go ahead whenever you're ready. I'll call your shots for you."

Jimmy took a deep breath, aimed and fired. A gout of water leaped out of the middle of the creek and sprayed into the air.

"By God, Jimmy, all my life I've heard the saying about

not bein' able to hit the broad side of a barn. You're the first person I ever come across that really can't."

"Don't laugh so hard, Longarm, you'll hurt yourself." Jimmy paused. "Come to think of it, go ahead and laugh hard as you damn please. Just don't look to me for sympathy when you bust your gut and end up lying there begging for mercy. You won't get any. No, sir, not from me you won't."

Longarm was still chuckling when he wiped the tears out of his eyes and said, "Try again, Jimmy. But this time aim for the creek. You might could hit the clay bank that way An' if you don't mind, I think I'd best stand behind you."

Jimmy laughed too. And raised his pistol again. They had plenty of ammunition to practice with and could get more when that was gone.

This time he did manage to hit the broad side of a barn.

Chapter 12

It was only a crossroads with a store and three houses, certainly not large enough to be considered a town, but it was coming dark and this was better than nothing. Longarm drew rein a quarter mile short of the settlement.

"I've noticed that the Dekins boys seem mighty comfortable in this country around here. Generally speaking, that is. My point is that we don't know where they might could have friends or where they wouldn't, so I'm thinking it'd be a good idea for you an' me to be just passing strangers. We won't say nothing about being deputy marshals and we won't give out any government vouchers."

Jimmy nodded. "That makes sense. But what, uh, what about . . . you know."

"Matter o' fact, I don't know. What the hell 're you talking about, Jimmy?"

"When we get there. To this place. What if there are, well, girls?"

Longarm grinned. "Kinda liked that, did you?"

"You know good and well that I did." A bulge in his

britches suggested that he was already anticipating a return to that particular form of pleasure.

"If there's a girl available, an' I don't know that there will be, but if there is one, go ahead an' enjoy yourself. I ain't your mama and I won't fault you for doin' what's natural." Longarm took the driving lines up and shook the little horse into a walk again. "Just don't expect the government to be paying for your fun." A few moments later he asked, "D'you need me to give you the borrow of a few dollars?"

"What? Oh, for . . . for that? No, I have money. But thank you."

"Sure, Jimmy. Any time."

"People are bound to wonder who we are and what we are doing here all banged up like this," Jimmy observed a moment later. What Longarm observed was that the kid's hard-on had subsided. That was good. He was paying attention to business.

"I'm open to suggestions," Longarm told him.

"We could be . . . oh . . . insurance adjusters. We are looking for a man to arrange the release of a settlement in his favor. But of course we cannot divulge any details. That information would be confidential. And we are in this condition because we had an accident. A runaway. It destroyed our carriage and killed the horse so we hired this buggy and are pressing on."

"Say, you ain't half bad at making up lies. Who are we looking for?"

Jimmy paused for only a moment before he said, "George McGrath. He is a farmer. Originally . . . hmm . . . I think our boy George is from Delaware."

"And who is it that we represent?"

"Delaware Life and Casualty."

"Is there really a company like that?"

"How the hell would I know?" Jimmy returned, his tone of voice suggesting he was grinning underneath those bandages.

"You're all right, Jimmy. Damned if you aren't."

When they reached the store Longarm pulled the buggy to a halt in front of it and said, "Why don't you go inside. See if there's a place we can get a bite to eat an' maybe someplace we can bed down for the night. I'll wait here if you don't mind. It's a real pain in the ass t' get down outa this rig with only one good leg under me."

"I'll be right back."

Jimmy was moving more easily now than when they first left Arnpelt. Either the healing processes were working or simply the act of moving around after so many days of inactivity appeared to be making him more comfortable. He hopped down from the buggy and disappeared inside the store. Longarm pulled out a cheroot and lighted it to enjoy while he waited for Jimmy to return.

Jimmy came back outside before Longarm had a chance to build a decent ash on the cheroot. "Pull around back. There's a shed where we can put the pony up. We will have to sleep in the straw. There aren't any rooms to be had."

"I've slept worse than that," Longarm said.

"We can take our supper with the gentleman who runs the store," Jimmy went on. "He lives in that house over there."

"And the other thing you was looking for?"

"The . . . oh." Jimmy chuckled. "Maybe. There, uh, there is a colored girl who works for the gentleman's wife. He said this girl sometimes will step out with a gentleman for twenty-five cents. Do you, uh . . . ?"

"She's all yours, Jimmy," Longarm said, sticking the cheroot into the corner of his mouth and taking up the driving lines. "The only place I'm steppin' out to tonight is that pile o' straw. I'm about all used up."

53

"If you're sure." He hesitated. "Could I ask you something, Longarm?"

"You can ask anything you like. Depends on the question do you get an answer or not."

"Have you ever been with, um, with a colored girl?"

Longarm laughed so hard the newly built ash tumbled off the tip of his cigar and dribbled down the front of his vest. "Yes, Jimmy, I been with colored girls. An' Indian girls an' Chinese an' Mexican and pretty much whatever else you're gonna find in this country, and I can tell you something true. Where it counts, Jimmy, they ain't no different, one from another. Some are good an' some ain't. Some will turn themselves inside out t' offer help to a total stranger while another will smile an' hug you an' rob you blind. The only thing you want t' remember kid is to treat them all decent an' you're be all right. And if you want a word of advice here, mind that you treat whores like they was ladies and they'll nearly always be straight with you for it."

"Even this colored girl?"

"Damn right, her too."

"All right. Uh . . . thank you."

"Sure." Longarm took the buggy around back, Jimmy walking alongside to the structure behind the store. The building was too large to be a shed and too small for a barn. There were two stalls and a storage lean-to. There was no loft but there was a grain bin in the lean-to and piles of both straw and grass hay under tarps at one side. Jimmy put an armload of hay and a quart or so of mixed grain into the bunk in one stall and spread straw on the floor of the other.

"You're useful t' have around, Jim."

"Just a minute and I will help you with that harness."

"Reckon I can get that, but it'd be good if you'd lead the

horse in. Don't know as I'd do so well handling him when I'm on these damn crutches."

"I'll take him. When we are all set here we can go over to the storekeeper's house. He said we can wait on the porch until he closes the store and joins us."

"Sounds fine t' me," Longarm allowed. "Sounds just fine."

Chapter 13

Supper was taken with the Reese family in a tiny but elegantly furnished formal dining room. Carl Reese the rural Kansas shopkeeper was a gray haired man of sixty or thereabouts. His wife Donna was probably twenty years younger. Wisps of gray highlighted her black hair. The woman wore a dress that was shiny with age but once had been the height of fashion, buttoned high at the throat and with puffy sleeves that narrowed to a tight fit at the wrists. Her hair was done in a prim and proper bun. Her mouth was as tight as the sleeves and as prim as the bun, to the point of being prissy. She did, however, have a set of the biggest tits Longarm ever saw outside a dairy barn. He was impressed.

The meal—a sort of pork stew with little meat but plenty of carrots and turnips—was served by a chubby colored woman of indeterminate age and bad teeth. Longarm assumed the maid did the cooking as well, the guess based on the fact that cornbread was served instead of biscuits. Jimmy the Kid was paying much more attention to the maid than to the food.

The woman was not all that much to look at but Longarm found himself trying to suppress an impulse to smile. He could remember how it was when he was just learning about just how varied the delights of the flesh could be. There hadn't been enough hours in the day to let him get enough, and back then he would cheerfully have fucked a bonfire if somebody had thrown a snake into it.

Since then, of course, he had matured. Now he would insist that someone hold the snake's head still.

Jimmy, he figured, was still eager enough to have a go at the bonfire. Maybe even without the snake.

The stew was fair, the coffee damn good and the dried apple cobbler afterward perfectly awful but it was all hot and filling and Longarm was grateful to have it. After the meal the gentlemen went out onto the porch to smoke. Longarm offered his; Reese accepted with pleasure but Jimmy declined.

"If you don't mind, sir, where, uh . . . when . . ."

"Right around behind the house here there's an out-house and a buggy shed. The girl sleeps in what used to be the harness room. She'll be there directly she finishes washing up the dishes. Don't you be going around there until it's full dark though. I wouldn't want my missus to see and to guess what's going on. Donna is what you might call of a delicate sensibility that way. She'd be right shocked, and it likely would cost me the services of a good worker."

"Thank you, sir."

"A man has needs, Mr. Wheelock. I can appreciate that."

Longarm had the notion that Carl Reese probably could deliver a report on the maid's performance and abilities in the sack if he were so inclined. Mrs. Reese struck him as the sort who would do her wifely duty when called upon. But without moving lest it just encourage more of that sort

58

of nastiness. And so long as it did not happen more than twice per annum.

The idea of that good matron taking a pecker into her mouth was enough to amuse hell out of him and such a suggestion very likely would have sent her running home to mama.

The gents sat on Reese's front porch smoking and relaxing in the cool of the evening until dark closed in around them. And until the sounds from inside the house subsided. The maid seemed to have finished washing the dishes. Mrs. Reese could be presumed to have gone off to bed. Alone and fixing to stay that way.

"If you would, uh, um . . ."

"It's perfectly all right, Mr. Wheelock, perfectly all right," Reese said.

"If you will excuse me, Carl," Longarm told him, "I think I'll turn in now too. Jimmy, before you go snorting off like a bull heading for the cow pen, whyn't you help me down these steps so's I don't trip an' fall." He grinned. "Was I t' do that I expect you'd have to carry me over to the barn and stay up tending to me the whole night long."

"I wouldn't want to risk that," Jimmy said.

"Breakfast will be a little past daybreak," Reese said. "I'll give you a call. We can settle up what you owe me then."

"That will be fine," Longarm said. "Just fine."

By then Jimmy already had him down the steps—half carried him there in his hurry to get away—and was already heading around toward the back of the Reese home.

"Thank you for the cigar, Mr. Long," Reese said.

"And I thank you for a fine supper." The meal hadn't actually been worthy of high praise, but it did not cost anything to be polite.

"Do you need help getting across the way, Mr. Long?"

"No, I'm fine, thanks. I'll see you in the morning, Mr. Reese."

"Until then, Mr. Long. Good night."

Longarm swung along on his crutches under an umbrella of bright stars, his belly warm and full. One belt out of the bottle of rye whiskey he liked to carry with him when he traveled and he would be good for the night, he figured.

Chapter 14

Longarm came instantly awake at the sound of footsteps outside the stall where he was sleeping. He had not been asleep very long. He was sure of that, and he was more than a little surprised that Jimmy the Kid would be returning so soon from his dalliance with the Reeses' maid. She must be a real disappointment in order for the kid to be back this quickly.

As young and vigorous as the kid was, Longarm really thought Jimmy would want to be rutting and experimenting the whole night through.

He was more than a little startled then when a shadowy figure was outlined against the bright moonlight outside the shed. His visitor seemed to be wearing a dress.

One of the neighbors come to borrow something from Reese's shed, he wondered. After all, there were two other houses at this nameless little crossroads settlement. Someone from one of them might want something here.

Might even have the notion to rob a pair of strangers passing through? Longarm slipped the Colt out of the holster he'd laid beside his head. A bit of precaution never hurts.

"Mr. Long?" The whisper was faint but clear. The voice sounded vaguely familiar. But improbable.

"Here," he said, putting his revolver back where it belonged. "Mrs. Reese?"

"Yes, it's me Donna." She reached out, groping and feeling her way forward, obviously unable to see inside the dark stall.

Longarm for his part could easily see her silhouetted against the pale outdoors. "Where are you, Mr. Long?"

"In the back o' the stall, ma'am. Is something wrong? Something happen to Jimmy?"

"Nothing is wrong, Mr. Long. Your friend will be occupied with Adele for hours and hours."

"You know where, uh . . ."

"Yes, of course. I know good and well where he is and what the two of them are doing." She reached the back of the stall.

"I'm to your right, ma'am."

"Yes. Thank you."

"You don't sound angry about, uh . . . you know."

"Angry? About Adele and your friend? Certainly not."

"Then if you don't mind me asking, ma'am, what is it you came t' tell me?"

"Oh, I did not come out here to *tell* you anything. I want to *show* you something."

"Yes, ma'am?"

"You really have to stop calling me ma'am, Mr. Long. My name is Donna. And thinking about those two, Adele and your friend . . . thinking about what the two of them are doing back there . . . it makes me half crazy, Mr. Long. It really does."

"I don't know as I ought to try an' stop them, Donna."

"Stop them? God, no. You misunderstand me. Thinking about them doing it makes me jealous, Mr. Long. I want it too. Carl, never . . . my husband is an old man, Mr. Long. And I am not that old a woman."

She spread her wrapper open and let it fall off her shoulders, leaving her standing over him naked.

Donna Reese was middle-aged and sagging. Those enormous tits, each one of the things the size of a milk bucket, drooped to her waist. Her belly bulged and her thighs were thick. She had unpinned her hair and it hung in ropy curls down to her butt. She was a big, severe, matronly woman, years older than Longarm and not exactly attractive.

But she was there. She was horny. The night was young. And he damn sure had nothing better to do.

"Down here, Donna," he said.

She knelt, hands still groping blindly as her eyes had not yet adjusted to the greater darkness inside the shed. "Where . . . ?"

"Here." He took her hand to draw her closer, then reached out and grasped a tit. He squeezed.

"Oh! I . . . oh." The woman practically lunged at him, throwing herself on top of him.

Her hands were all over him. Clutching, rubbing, hurrying to strip the clothes off him.

When she uncovered his cock she gasped with joy. "You're so big."

Longarm did not say anything. At that moment he couldn't. He was buried in the valley between her tits and was about half-smothered in there.

"So big," she repeated. "So big."

She apparently liked what she found there because this woman, who Longarm had thought was so prudish and proper, took his balls in one hand and his ass in the other while she did her level best to swallow his cock clear down into her belly.

And came near to accomplishing it, he suspected.

She was half-frantic with raw desire. Bobbing her head up and down on him and making eager, gobbling sounds. Slurping and sucking. Lifting him off his bed of straw so as to shove him in just that little bit deeper.

After a few moments she raised herself off him far enough to mumble, "Can you come more than once?"

"Sure. Why?"

She did not immediately answer but once again speared herself on Longarm's shaft.

He felt the swift gather of pleasure and then with little warning the explosion that sent what seemed like a pint of fluid spewing into Donna's mouth.

"Good," she whispered hoarsely. "It is nectar and it tastes so wonderfully good."

She went back to him then but more calmly, sucking with deliberate care until she was sure his erection was firm. Then she raised up and shifted position, straddling him and lowering herself onto him.

He felt the wet, hot grip of her flesh engulfing him. Felt too the press of her belly on his.

Donna braced herself over him and said, "Take hold of my breasts, Mr. Long. Take one in each hand and squeeze. Oh, yes. Harder, please. Yes. Hard. As hard as you can. Oh!"

She cried out and he could feel the contractions in her body as she reached a climax. Then another.

"Hurt them, Mr. Long. Dig your nails in. Hard. Yes-s-s-s-s-s!"

She came. Over and over again.

And so did he once she resumed the grinding and thrusting on top of him.

Donna Reese was not exactly the sort of woman Longarm had thought she was.

She used him, rutting over him until she was thoroughly sated, his pleasure seemingly unimportant to her.

She fucked him for what he guessed was two hours or more.

And then without any hint of warning she moved away from him, found her wrapper and stood to pull it on.

"Good night, Mr. Long."

And she was gone.

No, not exactly what he'd expected from Carl Reese's matronly wife.

Longarm slept extremely well that night.

Chapter 15

"I feel awfully guilty," Jimmy Wheelock told him the next morning as they were rolling south from Reese's crossroads.

"Guilty about being with that girl last night?" Longarm asked.

He reached for a cheroot and offered one to Jimmy, who shook his head and said, "No, thanks. I don't smoke. No, what I feel guilty about is being selfish with her. I should have brought her over so you could have had some too."

"That's mighty nice o' you, Jimmy. Thanks for thinkin' of me, but I, uh, I was comfortable enough last night."

"Yeah, I suppose when you get older, like you are, you kind of lose your yen for pussy and stuff."

Longarm smiled. But said nothing. Jimmy would learn that lesson in time. There was no point in trying to convince him of the truth beforehand.

"Say, could I change my mind about that cigar?" Jimmy asked a mile or so down the road.

"Sure, but I thought you didn't smoke."

"I don't. That is, I haven't. But I'm finding out that

some vices are pretty darn good. I think I'd like to try that one too."

Longarm chuckled and handed him one.

Jimmy fished a tiny pen knife out of his vest pocket, then realized he could not open it with one hand. The remaining fingers on his right hand were still wrapped inside a ball of bandages. "Say, could you, uh . . ."

"Bite it off," Longarm told him. "I could do it for you, an' I will if you want. But you can do more for yourself than you're allowing yourself to. More'n you think you can."

Jimmy nipped the twist off the end of the cheroot and jammed it into his mouth. Longarm struck a match and held it for him. The kid inhaled. And immediately went into a fit of coughing.

"You might wanta take it a little slower 'n that," Longarm suggested.

The kid drew on the smoke again, not so deeply this time. And began to smile. "Say, this isn't bad."

"What? You think I'd smoke them things as a punishment or something? O' course it's good. That's the only reason t' mess with them. Your mama tell you smoking is bad, did she?"

"As a matter of fact, she did," Jimmy admitted.

"No offense intended, but your mama is a woman. Women, most of them, got something against men having pleasures. Damn if I've ever figured out why, but they do. An' they'll lie to keep their sons from finding out about such as liquor and tobacco and the pleasures of a good blow job. One o' the things a man has t' learn, Jim, is to love women, your mama in particular, but take anything a woman says with a grain of salt."

Jimmy laughed.

Three hours later Longarm pulled the buggy to a half at

the entrance to a farm road that ran half a mile or so to a clump of stunted poplars that someday would make a nice windbreak. If they survived. At the moment they looked kind of scraggly.

"Lunch time?" Jimmy asked.

"Uh huh. If they'll feed us. Otherwise we'll see will the man let us water the horse before we head on down the road. We can eat jerky an' hardtack if we have to. But I'd ruther we didn't have to." He pointed the horse's nose onto the narrow track and picked it up into a jog.

"Hello the house," Longarm called as they wheeled into the farm yard. "Anybody home?"

There was no answer. Longarm and Jimmy sat in the buggy, the sun hot on their faces, for a minute or more and still there was no response from the house or from the barn.

"Hello," Longarm called again, louder this time. "Visitors here. Is anybody home?"

When there still was no answer he shouted, "We don't mean no harm. We'll step down t' draw a bucket o' water for this here horse, but that's all we got in mind. I want you should know that."

"The place is empty," Jimmy said.

"Uh huh. Except I seen a shadow pass behind that window on the front o' the . . . no, don't look, dammit. I seen something move behind the front window. Somebody's in there."

"Could be a cat left in the house," Jimmy said.

"Could be. I s'pose. But keep your hand close t' that shotgun under your leg just in case it ain't a cat nor some woman in there scared of strangers."

"You are a suspicious man, Longarm."

"Yeah, and I'm a live one too. Suspicion helps a man t' stay that way."

69

"Do you want me to get down and lead the horse over to the well?"

"No, stay put where you are. We'll drive over beside the well. Then we'll see." Longarm took up the lines and turned the buggy in a wide circle that brought them beside the well with the rig pointed back out toward the road. From the buggy seat they had a good view toward the farm house on their right and the barn to the left. The barn door was open a foot or so.

In a low voice Longarm said, "I want you t' get down now, Jim. Slow an' easy. Take the shotgun with you."

"Why?"

"Just do it. If anything happens, you're responsible for whoever is in the house. I'll take care o' the one in the barn."

"Someone is in the barn."

"I seen a shadow move an' what sure as hell looked like the muzzle of a rifle barrel. I'm thinking we might've drove into trouble here. Could be wrong, o' course, but let's us be ready for it if there is trouble."

There was trouble.

Jimmy got down from the buggy and reached back for his shotgun and a voice called out from the barn, "Don't touch that scattergun, mister."

A man wearing bib overalls and a slouch hat appeared in the partially open doorway. He had a Winchester rifle in his hands.

"We only came by to see could we get something to eat an' to water the horse," Longarm said loudly enough for his voice to carry to the house as well as the barn.

"You picked a bad day for it, mister. No, sir, this just ain't your day."

"We don't mean you any harm," Longarm said.

"No, but since you're here I expect me and my brother

70

got to mean you some. You walked in on something. Not your fault, but it is your problem. Now lay your guns down and empty your pockets. Both of you."

"Somehow, friend, I don't think you intend to stop with robbing us," Longarm said.

The man with the rifle shrugged. "Like I said, mister, it's just not your day. But I tell you what. Lay your guns down nice and easy. We'll take your money and tie you up. Somebody will come along to cut you loose by and by."

"That sounds fair enough. You have the drop on us. There isn't much we can do," Longarm said, "and we're peaceable men. We don't want no trouble." He turned toward Jimmy and in a very low voice said, "I'm fixing to drop this one. I figure his brother is inside the house. He's yours."

"You know I haven't been able to hit shit with this thing," Jimmy said.

"What are you two up to over there?" the man with the rifle demanded.

"Nothing. Just giving up," Longarm said in a loud voice, then to Jimmy added, "This 'd be a real good time for you to get in some more practice with your shotgun, Jimmy."

"But . . ."

"Aw hell, I got faith in you. Now if you'd excuse me for a second . . ."

Longarm's hand flashed and the big Colt .44 bellowed. The man with the rifle was hit in the belly. He jackknifed back from the open door and landed on his butt just inside the barn. His hand closed on the grip of his rifle, sending a bullet somewhere out over the farm fields. Longarm took his time and sent a second bullet into the fellow's upper torso, the slug going in low and ranging up through the chest cavity. The fellow jerked, his legs doing a macabre dance, and then he was still.

Longarm heard the dull roar of a shotgun blast and the sound of shattering glass. The buggy horse tried to bolt, and for a moment there Longarm had his hands full bringing it back under control.

"I think . . ." Jimmy began. The shotgun boomed again, and a voice cried out in pain. "There, dammit. I think I'm getting a little better with this now, Longarm."

"I knew you could handle it, Jimmy. Now help me down from here an' we'll go see what it is we stumbled into."

Longarm kept an eye on the house—he knew good and well the fellow in the barn was dead—while Jimmy collected Longarm's crutches and prepared to help him down to the ground.

Chapter 16

The one inside the house was dead too. Jimmy Wheelock's shotgun had taken off half his face and all the head that had been behind that part. It was a particularly ugly sight.

"Jesus!" Jimmy said. "I could've looked exactly like that. Jesus Christ."

"Count your blessings, Jimmy. You got tore up some but you're still a deputy an' you still got the sting in you."

Jimmy stood for some time staring down at the man he killed. Longarm suspected this was the first Jimmy shot dead. That was not something easily taken.

Longarm was in the middle of reloading the expended chambers in his Colt when he heard a sound from the back of the farm house. It was a sort of whimper. "Shit." He quickly shoved the last fat brass cartridge into the revolver and flicked the loading gate closed.

It was not easy handling the revolver and crutch at the same time but he managed as best he could, thumping across the puncheon floor with all the stealthy silence of a brass band on the Fourth of July. He was not going to sneak up on anybody until he got off these crutches, he realized.

73

The whimpering, accompanied by scratching noises, was coming from behind a closed door. Longarm gave his weight and balance to the left hand crutch and set the right one aside, leaning it up against the wall so he would have that hand free for his .44. He pressed the muzzle of the Colt against the door and pushed, shoving the poorly hung door open.

Someone inside the room began to sob when the door swung open. "D-d-don't h-hurt me."

Longarm pushed the door the rest of the way open and was greeted with the sight of a battered and bleeding woman, naked as the day she was born, tied hand and foot to a brass bedstead.

He rushed toward her but forgot for the moment the damned busted leg. Instead of going to her side he ended up sprawled on the floor.

"Shit!" he said again, this time loudly and with emphasis.

The woman had a scrap of cloth wrapped around her jaw. It was probably intended as a gag but did a piss poor job of it.

"You . . . don't hurt me. Stay away. Just . . . leave me alone. Please."

Jimmy must have heard or seen Longarm take a tumble because he was there in an instant. He dropped his shotgun onto a chest of drawers and knelt beside Longarm. "Are you all right?"

"Yeah. Fine. Help me up, Jimmy, then cut the lady loose, will you?"

Jimmy helped Longarm to his feet and retrieved the other crutch for him, then ran back into the front room. "Got to find a knife," he called over his shoulder. Longarm shrugged and pulled his own knife out. He sliced the heavy cord that bound the woman spread-eagled on the bed.

The woman was little more than a girl. Twenty years old

give or take a few, he guessed. She had blond hair and the firm breasts and flat belly of youth. She would have been exceptionally pretty if she were not covered with bruises and gashes and dried blood. Her face was puffy and her left eye was swollen almost completely closed.

She had been beaten and smears of blood at her crotch showed that she had been raped as well, probably very hard and repeatedly.

Longarm found a folded quilt at the foot of the bed. He managed to shake it out and was in the process of spreading it to cover the woman when Jimmy returned with a butcher knife in hand. The woman saw Jimmy, saw the knife in his hand, and passed out cold. Her eyes rolled back in her head and she went completely limp.

"What's wrong?" Jimmy asked. "What happened here?"

"Looks t' me like those brothers out there, Beezle and Bub, been brutalizing this poor lady."

Jimmy looked puzzled. "You know their names?"

"No, I . . . never mind. Look, this here is somebody's home an' I doubt it belongs to the lady alone. Either her husband is off on a trip somewheres an' those bastards knew he was gone or else they jumped him first before they started in on her. Is that shotgun o' yours loaded?"

"No, I . . . I guess I forgot."

Longarm's expression hardened. "You forget that at the wrong time, boy, and you could end up dead because of it. What I think you oughta do is go back out t' the buggy an' put fresh shells in that gun, then take a look in the barn. See if there's more than the one body in there. I shot the fellow by the door, but I'm thinking there might could be another that's longer dead."

Jimmy nodded and hurried out. Longarm looked around and spotted a pitcher and basin on a small table at the side of the bedroom. The pitcher was about half full. Longarm poured a little into the basin. He did not see a washcloth or anything he could use as one so he made do by pulling the lace doily off the table and soaking that in the cool water. Then he stumped back over to the bed and sat on the edge of it, careful not to touch the woman with his hip lest she think he was going to abuse her too. He used the wet lace to begin sponging the worst of the cuts on her face.

After a moment she came to. Her eyes went wide with fear.

"It's all right, miss. I'm a deputy U.S. marshal. I won't let nobody hurt you any more. That's a promise."

Chapter 17

Her name was Agatha Teeterbaum. She was—had been—a mail order bride from Maine. She had been married to Johan Teeterbaum less than a year.

"Johnny, he started farming here about twenty years ago. It is a good farm and he is a good farmer, but he was lonely. So he wrote to one of the agencies and they put us in touch. We wrote back and forth for several months. Then I . . . came out here. I loved it. It's nice here. Clean. And Johnny is such a good man. Where is he, marshal? Where is Johnny now?"

"We'll get into that later. Can you tell me about the men that hurt you? Were there just the two of them or were there others with them?" Longarm was frankly wondering if this pair might have been a part of the Dekins gang.

"There were . . . just the two. They came by two . . . or maybe it was three days ago. I don't remember for sure. Is that important?"

"No. Just tell us what happened, please." Between them he and Jimmy had her cleaned up a little. They changed the sheets on the bed and had her sitting up now, decently covered in a fresh nightgown and thick robe.

77

"They came . . . they came on foot. Carrying bundles wrapped in cloth."

"Were they wearing guns?"

"Oh, no. I don't think Johnny would have invited them to stay if they looked threatening. They just looked down and out. They asked if they could work for food. Cut wood or anything like that. Johnny can't stand to think of an animal going hungry and a person all the more so. He told them he could give them a few days of work if they liked. He needed help digging post holes, you see, for a hog pen he wanted to build.

"We fed them and let them sleep in the barn and then after breakfast . . ." She paused. "Yesterday? I'm really not sure. It all runs together in my mind, you see. It might have been yesterday but it could have been the day before."

"It doesn't matter," Longarm said. "Go on, please."

"It was after breakfast. I remember that for sure. The two of them and Johnny went out to start work for the day. They hadn't been gone long. I was . . . I was still washing the dishes. I heard someone at the door. It was . . . it was those men."

"Both of them?"

She nodded. "Yes. Both. They walked in like they owned the house. I asked them where Johnny was. I asked them what they wanted. They didn't say anything. One of them . . . hit me. With his fist like he was hitting another man. Hard. I fell down. The other one took me by the hair . . . my hair was pinned up at the time, of course. He took me by the hair and pulled me off the floor. Then he hit me too. They both did. For a while. Then . . . then they brought me in here. On my own bed. They ripped the clothes off me and they . . . did what they wanted."

Aggie Teeterbaum began to cry. "They did it over and over again. They took turns. They tied me up and they beat me and they burned me with cigars and they you know what they did to me. And they just kept at it. I really don't know how long it went on. A long time. Marshal, where is my husband? Where is Johnny?"

Longarm glanced at Jimmy, who had been the one who found a third body in the barn, just as Longarm expected. He turned back to the woman. "Your husband, ma'am. How old a man is he?"

"Johnny will be fifty-three next month," she said. There was probably a good thirty years difference between the husband and the wife. But that fit with what Jimmy said the dead man in the barn looked like. He was killed at a blow that split the back of his head open, struck down from behind by men he tried to help by taking them in and giving them food and work.

"I have, uh," Longarm cleared his throat and looked away. This was something he'd had to do too many times but he was not accustomed to it. Did not want to be. "I have to give you some bad news, Mrs. Teeterbaum."

"My Johnny is dead, isn't he?"

"Yes, ma'am."

"I . . . I knew that, I suppose. He would have come to me. He would have fought them. He would have tried to protect me."

"He did try an' protect you, missus. He surely did." It was a lie, he supposed. Johan Teeterbaum never knew he and his wife were in danger. They hit him from behind and Teeterbaum was dead before he could so much as know what was happening. But Longarm thought it would be a kindness in the years to come if his widow thought her Johnny died trying to protect her.

"D'you have neighbors, ma'am? Friends? Anybody we can take you to?"

"No, I . . . I will have to stay here. Someone needs to do the chores. See to the stock. Everything. I will be all right."

"Yes, ma'am. I'm sure you will." And if he did not believe that he at least wished that he could. "Jimmy, let's load the, uh, the deceased into that farm wagon I seen out beside the barn. We'll take them to town to be laid out an' buried proper." There was no way he and Jimmy alone, Longarm on crutches and Jimmy with only one hand, could dig three graves and take care of the dead.

Besides, those sonuvabitch killers did not deserve to be buried in the same ground as the man they murdered. Johan Teeterbaum should have a proper funeral. The pair of killers could be planted in Potter's Field with no stone and no names. Piss on them.

Longarm touched the brim of his Stetson. "If you will excuse us, ma'am?"

"Yes, marshal. Thank you. Both of you."

Chapter 18

Longarm drove the farm wagon with its load of three dead men. Jimmy followed in the buggy with Mrs. Teeterbaum beside him. Managing two driving lines with one hand was difficult, but fortunately the buggy horse was calm and reliable and Jimmy was able to accomplish the task for the slow, eight mile drive to town.

They took Aggie Teeterbaum to a friend's house, then Jimmy went by the church to alert the local pastor to this problem within his flock while Longarm found the undertaker, who was also the town barber, and dropped off his load there. They got together again at the town constable's office.

"You say you two are deputy United States marshals?" the constable said, giving them a blatantly skeptical looking over. Not that Longarm could blame him. He himself was on crutches with his leg in a splint, and Jimmy looked like an Egyptian mummy with the heavy bandage wrappings covering his head and right hand. Rather dirty bandage wrappings by now, Longarm noticed. They really needed to find a store where they could buy more.

"Yes, we are. Here's our credentials."

"Well I'll be damned. You don't look, uh. . . ."

"No, we don't," Longarm agreed. "We had a bit of a problem. Came out second best in a scrap up north. You wouldn't happen to have a doctor in town, would you?"

"Matter of fact, we do. Doc Northrup. I can show you where he lives. It's easy enough to find."

"All right, thanks."

"Is there anything you want me to do?" the town constable asked.

"Yes, there is. I'd like you to go through the wanted flyers and see if our two dead men have any reward money on them. If there is anything, I'd like you to file for it and give the money to Mrs. Teeterbaum. Would you do that, please?"

"Now that is something I'd be pleased to do. Indeed it would."

"One other thing then," Longarm said. "Have you heard anything about the Dekins gang being in the vicinity? We heard they were somewhere around here and to tell you the truth we'd like to avoid them, the condition we're in and everything."

"Was it them that banged you up like this?"

Longarm shrugged.

"I heard there was some sort of dust-up with them. Up in Arnpelt, was it?"

Longarm nodded. Jimmy added, "Yes, damn them."

"I don't blame you for wanting to stay clear of them now," the constable said. "Far as I know though you should be safe enough around here. I haven't heard of any of them being in my town."

"That's good," Longarm told him. And he meant it. He wanted to encounter the gang again but on his own terms this time and in a place that was of his choosing. The

Dekins bunch had been in control in Arnpelt. Now Longarm wanted to be the one with his hand on the reins.

"If you would excuse us now, constable?"

"Will you be staying here long?"

"Overnight, I expect. We'll be at the hotel if you need us."

When they went outside Jimmy said, "I want to do some shopping, Longarm, but I'll need your help to do what I want."

"All right."

A mercantile let them replenish the few supplies they had used along the way. In addition to the foods, Jimmy selected a cheap hacksaw, a small hand saw, a fine rasp and a brace and bit. "I need a wood bit with that," he told the storekeeper. "A quarter inch or so will do. Oh, and I need a couple piggin strings if you have any already cut or a thong. Something on that order anyway."

"I can fix you up," the storekeeper said. And did.

Longarm asked no questions. He figured the kid would tell him sooner or later. After all, he'd said he needed Longarm's help with whatever this was.

"Let's go over to the doctor's office next," Longarm suggested.

"Are you feeling sick or something?"

"No, but you need to have those bandages changed. You've got food stains all around your mouth, and there's some seepage leaking out from your bad eye. It won't hurt to have everything looked at."

Longarm stayed in the outer office while Jimmy saw the doctor. He did not particularly want to see what lay beneath the bandages. He did think Jimmy looked much better when he came out a half hour or so later in spanking fresh wrappings. The openings over his mouth and good eye were larger, and right hand was no longer wrapped.

The stumps where his thumb and missing fingers had been were red and crusted with scabs, but at least this way he could get some use out of the remaining fingers. His posture and gait suggested Jimmy was feeling pretty good.

"How'd it go?" Longarm asked.

"The doctor said that barber back in Arnpelt did as good a job as he could've and maybe better. He thinks given time I'll heal up well enough to go out in public without bandages or a mask or anything."

"Good. What about your eye?"

"Oh, that's gone. He said there is nothing that could have been done about it."

"Tough."

Jimmy only shrugged. As far as Longarm could see there was no self-pity in the gesture either.

"What about these tools then?" Longarm asked.

"I'll bring them up to the hotel room. We can use them after supper if you don't mind. I wouldn't bother you if I didn't have to, but I don't think I could use the brace and bit with one hand. Although maybe . . . if I lean on the brace with my shoulder and turn it with my left hand . . ."

"I'll help you do whatever it is you want done, Jimmy."

That chore, as Longarm learned after supper, was first to cut the barrels of Jimmy's shotgun back just in front of the wooden hand guard, until there was very little tube remaining past the length of the shotgun shells. The useable barrel length was not more than a handspan, call it nine inches or so. Longarm used the hacksaw to cut the twin tubes down.

"What next?" he asked.

Jimmy handed him the small wood saw. "I'd like you to cut the stock off so it's no more than a pistol grip."

"Then smooth the edges with the rasp, is that it?"

Jimmy nodded.

A rather nice piece of walnut was quickly reduced to the size and shape that Jimmy wanted.

"And the brace?" Longarm asked. "What is that for?"

"I want you to drill a hole at the bottom of the pistol grip. Right about here." He pointed. "I'll put this thong through there and use it to hang the gun off my shoulder. Or across my chest might be better. It wouldn't be so likely to slip off that way. Anyway, I want to carry the gun hanging barrel-down on my left side so I can get to it in a hurry. I'll still want to carry my revolver too, but I think it's going to be an awfully long time before I'm accurate with a pistol. The shotgun will be quicker to master."

"We'll stop in the morning and get a case of shells for it then," Longarm said. "If that is the gun you intend t' rely on you'd best spend some time with it. Have you thought about the recoil? A 12 gauge has plenty of kick, and you'll not get any help from your right hand except to lay the barrels over it."

"I thought about it. I'll just have to learn to handle it. Besides, that is one of the reasons I want to keep it hanging on a strap. If the damn thing flies out of my hand I won't have lost it. I can just grab it up again and I'll be back in business."

"You're a gutsy little son of a bitch, Jimmy. More'n I ever gave you credit for."

"Coming from you, Longarm, I take that as a compliment."

"Good 'cause it was intended as one. Now tell me how you want the grip on this thing shaped. It oughta fit your hand as best we can manage."

Chapter 19

Longarm stopped a quarter mile short of the sprawling, sandstone fort on the Pawnee Fork of the Arkansas.

"Is something wrong?" Jimmy asked.

"That's what I'm wondering. Last time I was here this place was an anthill of activity. Soldiers every-damn-where pretending t' be useful. Now all I can see is a little smoke coming outa that chimney yonder."

"Could they all be out on patrol or something?"

"Damned if I know," Longarm admitted. "Not likely though. There's always been mostly infantry stationed here an' them mostly used for escort duty, accompanying wagon trains along the Santa Fe Trail. O' course the trail ain't used so awful much any more. The railroads carry most everything nowadays. There just ain't so many wagons carrying long distance freight."

"The fort hasn't been abandoned though," Jimmy said. "That is a garrison flag on display."

"Yeah. It's odd though. Only one way t' find out for sure." Longarm took up the lines and shook the horse into a walk. "Remember though. Far as anybody at Larned

87

needs t' know, we're travelers passing through on our way to Santa Fe. If the Dekins boys is meeting somebody here we don't want to tip our hand to anybody. We damn sure don't want them t' know there's three-fourths of a deputy U.S. marshal waiting for them."

Longarm grinned and Jimmy laughed outright.

"That's us," the kid agreed. "Three quarters of one human."

"Hell, Jimmy, good as you're getting with that shotgun o' yours we might even make one whole person between us."

"I still need practice with the pistol though."

Longarm's grin returned. "Ain't that what you'd call a understatement? I swear when it comes to the pistol you'd be better off throwing it at somebody than trying t' shoot him with it."

"True enough," Jimmy agreed.

The rolled into the fort and stopped in front of the headquarters building. There was no one in sight.

"What do we do now?" Jimmy asked.

"Get down an' make ourselves to home, I suppose. There has to be somebody here though what with the flag and smoke coming from the mess hall."

"Stay where you are while I get your crutches and help you down."

It galled Longarm to have to depend on Jimmy for assistance, but it was still damn-all difficult for him to get into or down from the buggy. Between them they managed however.

"What about the horse?" Jimmy asked when they were both afoot.

"There's plenty o' room here for wagons passing through. Hell, that's why the fort was built. I don't know how it is now, but before the railroad got put through it was the law that every wagon train on the trail had t' have an escort for passage west of Larned. We'll put our buggy in the wagon park an' turn the horse into one o' the corrals."

"I'll do that," Jimmy volunteered, "while you find somebody to report to."

Longarm nodded and made his way toward the one building that showed any sign of life. A neatly lettered sign over one of the doors confirmed that the solidly built building was the post mess hall. Longarm was only a few steps short of reaching it when a man wearing a very sloppy uniform appeared in the doorway. The fellow was graying and grizzled. He hadn't shaved in some time and his shirt was unbuttoned and hanging outside his trousers. There were sergeant's stripes on his sleeves.

"What do you want, mister?" the sergeant said by way of greeting.

"Me and my friend are traveling through," Longarm said, leaning on his crutches. "We had an accident an' are kinda banged up. Thought we'd rest here for a bit before we tackle the rest o' the road."

The sergeant grunted but said nothing.

"Mind if I ask you something?" Longarm said. "I was past here once before. The place was a lot busier then. What happened to all the soldiers that used t' be here?"

The sergeant scratched himself, then said, "There no troops here any more. They've all been moved to other posts. All but me and a guard detail to watch over the place and keep people like you from stealing things until the government figures out what to do with it."

"That's the whole garrison?"

The sergeant nodded. "Me and six soldiers under my command." He turned his head a little and raised his voice. "Them six and one cook who can't boil water worth a shit."

"Go fuck yourself, Johnson," a voice responded from inside the mess hall.

89

"Would it be possible for us to shelter in the barracks and take our meals with you while we're recuperating for the rest of the journey?" Longarm asked. "We would be willing to pay, of course."

The sergeant scratched his balls again, then dug his fingernails into the fur on his chest. "You say you can pay?"

"Yes, we'd be happy to."

Johnson grunted. "How many of you is there?"

"Two. And one horse."

"One horse between you?"

"That's right. We're traveling in a buggy."

"Two of you and a horse. All right. Dollar a day then." He paused and when Longarm did not flinch at that price said, "For each of you. Fifty cents for the horse. There's hay in the stable. You can have some of that. No grain though. They took all that with them when they left."

"Two dollars and a half per day. That sounds fine. How's about I give you ten dollars now. If we stay longer than four days I'll cover however long we're here."

"Fine," Johnson said. "Come inside if you like. We're having dinner now. I expect there's some left that you can have." He turned his head again. "Did you hear that, Boggs? You're cooking for two more while these gents is here."

"I have extra work to do and you take the profit. You really are a bastard, Johnson," Boggs returned.

"Shut your yap, Boggs, and do what you're told."

"Up yours, Johnson."

Jimmy joined Longarm and they went inside the mess hall. The men in this caretaking detail, they found, were all old soldiers, probably marking time until their retirement. And most of them were fuck-ups, Longarm judged by the dark places on their sleeves where stripes used to be but were no longer. They were men who had been dumped here so their units could get rid of them, he guessed.

They were slovenly and graying and obviously did not much concern themselves with military discipline.

But despite what Johnson claimed, Pvt. Boggs could damn sure cook. He managed to make even army rations taste good, and that was quite an accomplishment.

At least they would not go hungry, Longarm saw, while he and Jimmy waited here for the Dekins bunch to show up.

Chapter 20

"What do you think?" Jimmy asked when they were alone in a cottage that had once been an officer's living quarters. Sgt. Johnson, they'd learned, had established himself in the house that had been the post commander's quarters. The enlisted men of the detail were scattered inside the barracks buildings in housing that originally was assigned to senior non-commissioned officers.

"I think this isn't exactly what I expected," Longarm said. "One thing I'm sure of, though, is that Bob an' Brad Dekins aren't here. There's no chance they could get lost in a crowd this size. So I reckon we sit tight an' wait. They'll come to us."

"Do you think Dutch and Carl are onto them by now?"

Longarm shrugged. "There's no way t' tell, but they was going in the opposite direction the last we knew. It'd be good if they was to show up, but I ain't gonna count on it. No, whatever happens here, Jim, I expect it's up to the two of us."

"The three-fourths, you mean."

"Yeah," Longarm said with a grin. "But that three-fourths of a human has a sting." The grin grew wider. "Comes to that, Jimmy, I can whack 'em with a crutch while you thump them with your stump."

"You really know how to inspire confidence, don't you."

"Leadership ability is one o' my finer qualities."

There was no retreat formation called by the caretaker detail. Late in the afternoon one of the privates ambled out to the parade ground and hauled the flag down without ceremony. Shortly afterward Boggs clanged a call to supper on an iron triangle hanging by the mess hall door.

Longarm and Jimmy joined the soldiers who were gathered in a very small cluster close to the kitchen where a few lamps spread light into that end of a building designed for the feeding of two hundred or more at one sitting. The remainder of the long room was dark and cavernous.

The soldiers sat at the table closest to the kitchen, each of them in the same places where they had been sitting at lunchtime, their places occupied by force of habit, Longarm guessed. He and Jimmy settled at a nearby table rather than intrude on the soldiers.

Boggs and one of the men brought out steaming bowls of short ribs cooked in sauerkraut.

"This is good," Longarm said, turning toward the soldiers' table. "Where d'you get fresh meat though? This damn sure ain't the salt pork and bacon I expected."

"There's some Injuns that come by a couple times a week. They trade us meat for salt and sugar," one of the men answered.

Another soldier added, "That ain't all they bring." His comment brought a round of laughter from the others, even from Johnson.

"An' what's that supposed to mean?" Longarm said.

"You'll see."

"Oh, go ahead and tell the man. Civilians get horny too.

At least I think they do. I can't remember that far back, not for sure."

"Shit, Boston, you can't remember last week, never mind back before you joined up."

"I can remember how to whip your ass any time I take the notion," the man called Boston snapped, suddenly testy.

Longarm guessed that these few men had been isolated here long enough to have just about a bellyful of each other. "Indians?" he said, changing the subject before an argument could get started among the men. "I didn't see any Indians camped close by."

"They're upstream a ways. Johnson wouldn't let them set up too close. There's not enough of us to keep them from stealing the place down to the walls if there was too many of them around. But they come by now and then to trade and, uh, whatever."

"What he's getting at," Boston put in, "is that some of those bucks will swap you the use of a woman for a pint of whiskey or a twist of tobacco."

"Didn't you boys luck into some good duty," Jimmy said. "For a little whiskey, you said?"

"That's right. There's some in the storehouse. We can fix you up with a pint if you'd like."

"I think I would," Jimmy told him. "Thanks."

"Next time the Injuns come by. We'll take care of you."

"Just don't pick the fat little squaw in the red dress," Sgt. Johnson advised. "The little cunt gave me the crabs."

"They aren't so bad, most of them. And they don't smell bad. I always thought Indians stunk but they don't."

"That's because they take baths, Worden. You might take a lesson from that."

"When the army tells me to bathe I'll obey the order, Taylor. Until then leave me the fuck alone."

"This seems like a pretty cushy deal you boys have

here," Longarm said, again wanting to divert their attention before a fight broke out.

"Oh, it ain't always so good."

"Now that's the damn truth. It was a bitch here before the Injuns started to show up."

"That was recent was it?" Longarm asked.

"Yeah. They've been here for just a few weeks. A month maybe. They're starting to gather for some kind of pow-wow or something."

"Nobody's exactly told us what's going on."

"If the army wants you to know, it will tell you."

"That's if the damn army remembers we're here. I swear I think maybe they've clean forgot about us."

"They remember well enough to pay you, don't they?"

"Sure. Every three or four months. Bastards. They don't even pay us regular."

"You can walk away any time you want, Worden. Walk away and leave your pension behind if you like. Nobody here will try and stop you."

"Fuck you too, Billup. What are you looking at, Johnson? Fuck you and the horse you rode in on."

These soldiers were like a bunch of bickering old women, Longarm realized. They were prickly and quick to grumble but were not likely to take things further than heated words. Rolling around on the ground battering each other was for the young and the vigorous. None of these men were either young or full of vigor.

He was interested in the fact that a group of Indians were gathering outside Fort Larned, however. They were likely to be here for a reason, and he could not help but wonder if that reason had anything to do with the visit planned by the Dekins boys.

"Say, can we get seconds?" Jimmy asked. "This is awfully good."

"Help yourself," Boggs answered from the other table. He pointed toward the kitchen. "There's a big pot on one of the stoves in there. Take whatever you like."

"Do you want more, Longarm?"

"Can you handle two bowls?" He gestured toward what remained of Jimmy's right hand.

"Not at once but I can make two trips," Jimmy answered. "I can handle anything I need to. Anything."

"Then yeah, I'd like a refill too, thank you." If he kept on thinking like that the kid was going to be just fine, Longarm thought. Just fine.

Chapter 21

"I'm gonna need the buggy hitched up this morning," Longarm announced after breakfast.

"I thought you said we would stay here and wait for them to come to us."

"The sergeant said there's a band of Indians camped upstream. I want t' go see who they are an' why they're here."

"They're Indians. They are all over this country, aren't they?" Jimmy asked.

Longarm pulled out a cheroot, offered one to the kid, then lighted up himself before he answered. "There used to be plenty of them around here," he said. "They used t' put sentinels on top of Pawnee Rock . . . remember when we come past it the other day; it's high an' looks out over a whole lot of territory. Hell, Pawnee Rock and all those Indians is the reason the army built this post to begin with. There was that many attacks on the bull trains in the Santa Fe trade. The army came here to protect commerce not folks, by the way.

"There was some mighty important pow-wows and treaties signed right here too, back in the old times, and there was some awful bloody campaigns mounted out of Larned back then. But the buffalo been killed off now an' settlers are taking up land over most o' Kansas from here on east. All the Indians been pushed west an' north. Even the wild tribes in the unassigned lands down south don't come up here much nowadays. So it makes me real curious about why there'd be a band of 'em going into camp up here again."

"Surely it couldn't have anything to do with the Dekins gang, could it?" Jimmy asked.

"Damn if I know any way it could, but I want to find out. After all, we got two groups here or on the way here, to a place neither one of them would normally be. Could be coincidence." Longarm paused for a moment to exhale a slow stream of smoke, then grunted. "If you believe in coincidence." He looked Jimmy in the eye. "Jimmy, I don't believe in coincidences. Not worth a damn, I don't."

Jimmy picked up his shotgun and slipped the thong over his head so the gun dangled free at his left side. "I'll get the wagon."

"I want you t' get the wagon, but you can leave the scattergun. You ain't coming with me."

"But. . . ."

"I got something I need you t' do, Jim. I want you to keep yours eyes . . . well, the one you got left, that is . . . want you to keep your eye open an' both ears too. The Dekins boys are coming here to meet somebody, and that somebody pretty much has to be the sergeant or someone in his caretaker detail. I don't want you asking questions or calling attention to yourself in any way. Remember, these boys don't know what you and me do for a living an' I don't want them to. So I want you to observe every-damn-thing nice and quiet like. See if you can spot anything suspicious that might point a finger at whoever our boy is."

"All right. I can do that. Would it be all right if I drink with them or play some cards, anything like that?"

"Hell, kid, if you can get some of them into a game, you go right ahead. That might could be a good way to get their tongues loose."

"All right, I'll see what I can do. In the meantime, I'll go fetch the buggy."

Longarm nodded and reached for his crutches. He wondered if Johnson had any tobacco in the post supplies that he would be willing to let Longarm have. He wanted to show up at the Indian encampment with some sort of present to offer, and he would rather not have to give away his own dwindling supply of cheroots.

As far as Indian encampments went, this one was kind of pathetic. There was only seven lodges grouped tight together in a clearing that would have accommodated half a hundred. Kiowa he thought, judging by the markings painted onto the lodge skins.

There had been a time when even a tiny band of Kiowa would be cause enough for panic. There had been a time when the tribe had the reputation of being thieving, murdering, blood-thirsty sons of bitches. And that was a reputation they damn well earned.

Like the Blackfoot before them and more recently the Lakota, however, nowadays the Kiowa had been tamed. Their war leaders were either dead or in prison cells, and the people depended on reservation lands and government handouts to get along.

Those Kiowa reservation lands, if Longarm remembered correctly though, were down by Fort Sill. *Not* in the vicinity of this empty and crumbling post that Larned had become.

Tame Indians, Longarm reflected as he drove the buggy into the ring of tipis. Tame but not cowed. These Kiowa had conceded the power of the U.S. military but they still had balls. They remembered the way things used to be. That was made perfectly clear by the presence in the center of their camp of a seemingly insignificant display of poles planted in the earth.

Scalp poles, they were, commemorating past Kiowa victories. The poles were decorated with the feathers of predatory birds . . . and with the dried scalplocks of conquered enemies.

More than a few of those scalps had hair that was blond or brown and even several, probably quite prized for their rarity, that were red. They were the scalps of white men, perhaps soldiers, perhaps buffalo hunters.

Longarm pulled the buggy to a halt and remained on the seat, waiting for someone to come welcome him as custom required.

Chapter 22

For a moment there Longarm had the very unpleasant sense that he had fucked up. The faces that showed in the lodge entries were all of warriors. There seemed to be no children in the camp. And, now that he thought of it, no dogs either. There should have been plenty of both if this were an ordinary sort of movement by the band. Instead all he saw were men. Then, gradually, he began to see a few females among the Kiowa.

Even their presence was odd however. There were old men but no old women with them. Only young women with energy enough to do the camp work, and there seemed an unusual number of warriors crammed into each lodge. Eight or ten in each tipi, Longarm saw, plus the females to handle the labor and the cooking.

The men were not painted for warfare and presumably—hopefully—would not be inclined to murder passing strangers. Not this close to the fort anyway. Larned was only a mile and a half or so downstream.

Of course that would be too far if the Kiowa decided to

jump him. Johnson and his badly outnumbered detail of aging soldiers would not be able to arrive in time to mount a rescue even if they tried.

If the Indians really wanted to take another scalp for their pole. . . .

"Hello," Longarm called. He reached behind the seat and brought out a bundle of goods he had obtained from the post supplies before setting out. "I brought presents."

One of the men, this one much younger than most of the warriors, stepped forward. "What do you want to buy here? You want meat? You want souvenirs?"

"Your English is mighty good," Longarm said.

"So is yours. You do not answer my question. What do you want to buy with your presents?"

"If you speak that good you should know there's a difference between a present an' a payment. I brought some t'bacco as a gift, not t' buy anything with."

"Why?"

Longarm shrugged. "The soldiers said there were Indians here. I wanted to meet you. Get a look at some real plains Indians." He smiled. "Wanted t' see if all those pictures in the magazines are accurate."

"Are you satisfied now that you have seen a genuine savage?" He waved his hand to encompass the crowd of silent onlookers.

"Sure. Uh, what tribe are you?"

"Kiowa."

"I thought your reservation was down south o' here."

"It is. This is not our reservation."

"Oh. You just come up here t' sell some meat t' those soldiers, did you?"

"There is a reason for us to be here."

"Mind if I ask you something?"

"You may ask."

"Your English. It really is awfully good. How'd you learn it?"

"My father was a great man. He did not want me to go to the white man's prison. He wanted me to learn. He sent me to live with a missionary family. Then I went to the Carlisle School. You have heard of it?"

"Yes, I have. They say it's a good school."

"They lie. The Carlisle School would pretend that white men and red are the same. I learned enough to know that this is not so. So I came home. I am not white. I am Kiowa. I have no shame of my people." He frowned. "I said that wrong. I am not ashamed of my people. Yes. That is better English now."

"May I ask your name?"

"I am Talking Bird, son of Satanta."

"Satanta? I have heard of your father."

"White men everywhere have heard of Satanta. There was a time when they trembled at his name. Little children were warned to be good or Satanta would come in the night and kill them."

"And would he have?"

Talking Bird nodded solemnly. "Yes. He would have killed them every one."

"My name is Custis Long," Longarm said. "Would you accept this gift from me, Talking Bird?"

"You want nothing in exchange?"

"No. I heard the giving of a gift was the proper thing to do when visiting a Kiowa village. That is why I brought it."

Talking Bird grunted. He turned and called out something and one of the young women darted forward. She bowed her head and dropped her eyes when she approached the buggy. Talking Bird took the package of tobacco and handed it to her with instruction in their own tongue, then the girl ran back to one of the tipis where there were a number of gray-haired men gathered to peer at this white intruder.

"Are you hungry?" Talking Bird asked.

Longarm nodded.

"Come. Eat." Without waiting for an answer Talking Bird turned and strode away. At one of the tipis he stopped to say something. A moment later a different young woman came to take charge of Longarm's horse and buggy.

Longarm climbed down to the ground and got his crutches, then followed in the direction Talking Bird had gone, leaving the girl to take care of the rig.

It occurred to him as he gimped slowly along that Talking Bird might not particularly like whites. After all, he was the son of Satanta, one of the Kiowas' war leaders. The man had indeed been a scourge from Kansas all the way down to Mexico. That was only warfare though, and a warrior takes his chances whenever he chooses to go on a raid.

The thing that might well twist Talking Bird's gut was that his father died in a U.S. Army prison. Or maybe it was a State of Texas prison. Longarm couldn't remember which, and he did not suppose it really mattered all that much.

What might well matter to Talking Bird was that Satanta was brought to earth, dragged away in chains and locked up in a cage. The war chief could not abide by the indignity of that. Once it became clear that he would have to spend the remainder of his life behind bars Satanta committed suicide.

Longarm rather hoped that Talking Bird or these other Kiowas did not decide this would be a right dandy time to get a little revenge on a white man.

Chapter 23

The meal was a thin stew of meat, wild onions, greens and rice all boiled together and eaten from wooden bowls without benefit of spoons or other utensils. Longarm ate as his hosts did, more or less drinking from the side of the bowl and using his fingers to shovel the chunky bits into his mouth. They ate sitting cross-legged on blankets around the ashes of last night's fire. The food had been cooked somewhere else and was served by several of the young women who scurried in and out of the lodge in silence.

When he was done Longarm rocked back, swallowed a mouthful of air and let out a roaring belch. The tonal quality might have been subject to criticism but it was hell for loud, a belch a man could be proud of.

He noticed that several of the older men, who had been talking among themselves throughout the meal, nodded with approval so he did it again, the second eruption decent if not quite as magnificent as the first had been.

"Talking Bird, please thank the grandfathers for their hospitality."

Talking Bird spoke in their native language for a moment and got back a number of comments from his elders, then he turned to Longarm. "They like you, Custis Long. You are welcome in our villages. They think you are no stranger to this land or to our people."

"I am not a stranger here," Longarm admitted, "but I don't know the Kiowa well."

"For a white man you have manners," Talking Bird said. "You do not place yourself between the people and the fire and you do not stare at our women."

"That would be rude," Longarm agreed.

"Whites do this anyway."

"They don't know any different, most of 'em. They don't mean t' be rude."

Talking Bird and one of the old men had a brief conversation, then in English Talking Bird said, "You had a reason to come to us. You are not a . . . a, uh. . . ."

"Tourist?" Longarm suggested.

"Thank you, yes. You are not a tourist."

"Your grandfather is right. I came because I am curious why you are here. All the more so now that I see your camp. You are not a village on the move. You brought girls to serve you, but your women and your children are wherever your village is. You have no dogs with you and only a small herd of ponies. These things make me curious."

"We are from many villages, many bands," Talking Bird said. "We who come here represent our people. We come to collect the reparation, here at this place where once a treaty was signed."

"Reparation?"

"It was learned that some of the white father's agents stole from our people. Food that was meant for us was sold to white thieves. Cattle to feed our babies and our grandmothers was paid for but never delivered. These things happened, Custis Long."

"I believe you, Talking Bird. I am sorry that this is so."

The Indians spoke among themselves again, then Talking Bird said, "When we learned of this, there was bad feeling among our people. Some of the men wanted to return to the ways of war. They said if we are to die anyway, let us die as men fighting the enemy and not as cowards who wither and blow away."

Longarm was silent for some time, showing respect by pondering what was said before he spoke again. "I have always heard that the Kiowa are warriors. This is honorable. What makes me sad is thinking that your people and mine must be enemies. I hope this does not happen again."

"We talked of these things. We sent our agent away and talked with a commissioner who came to us from Washington City. This agent said the white father wanted to make things right for us. He agreed to give us a reparation payment."

"That is good," Longarm said.

"He said it will be paid here, where the treaty was made." Talking Bird's chin came up and his eyes flashed with a fierce pride. "My father Satanta signed that paper. My father and Satank and his great friend Kicking Bird who I honored when I chose my own name."

"I have heard of these men. They were great warriors. Fine enemies," Longarm said. He did not belabor the obvious point that these great Kiowa warriors got their asses royally kicked by the United States Army. Or that of the men who signed that treaty, the ones who continued to fight were dead now.

"That is why we are here, Custis Long. We come to collect what is ours. Then we will go back to our homes. There will be no more war between your people and mine."

"Where are the men who will drive the cattle for you?" Longarm asked. "Where are the wagons to carry the foods that are promised?"

"We have learned, Custis Long. This time we are not asking for commodities that can be sold away or cattle too sick to walk such as have been given to us in the past. We told the commissioner we will take our reparation in gold. With gold we can buy the foods that please us and cattle to give the strength of their meat."

Longarm nodded. "That is wise," he said.

What he was thinking, though, had nothing to do with wisdom. And much to do with Bob and Brad Dekins.

Reparations would be brought here and paid here, would they? In gold?

No wonder the brothers were on their way to Fort Larned.

It occurred to Longarm too that Talking Bird said the tribe had been on the verge of a return to the warpath. If they did not receive the promised reparations they might very well decide to break out and launch one last wild, maniacal raid across the entire southwest.

An uprising by an enraged Kiowa nation could result in the slaughter of countless civilians before the army could bring things under control again. Hell, the north and the west of Texas were being settled now. Ranchers, even farmers were streaming onto the land now that the threat of Indian depredations was removed.

Or *should* have been removed.

He brought up none of this now though. He thought about it, worried about it, but all he said to Talking Bird was, "I am glad there is peace between our peoples now."

"Yes. There is peace."

But outside this lodge where they sat now for a peaceful dinner, the scalps of white and Indian alike dangled from the scalp poles and fluttered softly in the breeze.

Chapter 24

Now that Longarm had been accepted as a guest, the custom of the plains tribes was that he was free to stay as long as he wished. Oddly, even if he had been an enemy of the Kiowa he could have stayed among them without fear as their guest. Of course had he been an enemy, as soon as he chose to leave the village he would have been fair game and they would kill and scalp him without a qualm.

As it was he presented no threat and was no enemy. He could stay in complete safety and had to ask no one's permission to do so. He needed to make no announcement or apology, he could simply choose to remain however long he pleased then walk away without comment or explanation. The tribes were big on individual freedoms. Much more so in a way than the white culture.

Longarm stood and went outside to relieve himself in the weeds beside the river, then ambled back into the circle of lodges. A group of men were sitting in dappled sunshine playing the game of Hand, that most simple of games. Seemingly simple anyway. Deceptively simple in truth.

The game was played with one small stone and two participants. One man would take the stone and hold his hands behind his back. He could pass the stone from hand to hand however he wished and when he was ready hold both closed fists out in front of him. The problem was then for the other player to guess which hand held the stone. If he found it, he won; if that hand were empty, he lost.

The game was simple. Sure it was. Players gauged how tightly the other closed his fist. Judged his expression. His eye movements. The sweat on his brow.

And the game could be deadly serious. Longarm heard the tale—perhaps true, perhaps apocryphal—about a player at a water hole who encountered a warrior from another tribe. The two entered a friendly game of Hand, the first warrior steadily losing and wagering literally everything he owned until he sat naked before the other—yet he still believed he could win. Owning nothing of value he could wager he bet his own scalp as the stake in one final contest. He would win all or lose everything including his own life. The man lost and with a sigh meekly submitted to the taking of his scalp.

The tribes, it was said, honored the losing player as a man of great courage and principle.

Longarm tended to think the fellow had been one crazy son of a bitch. But he could see the Indians' point. The warrior had indeed been a man of much honor.

Longarm edged into the circle of players and nodded. Then emptied his pockets to find stakes he could place when it came his turn to hold the stone or to find it.

"Talking Bird, could I talk t' you for a minute please?"

The young Kiowa said something to the men he was with—excusing himself or possibly explaining what Longarm said—then followed a few steps away so they could have a little privacy.

"I haven't been properly introduced t' everybody," Longarm said, "and I'd like to make the acquaintance of the headman of this village."

Talking Bird looked a little puzzled. "I have told you, Custis Long, that this is not really a village. We are from different bands, come together here for the one purpose. The whole tribe did not come. That would have been difficult so these were chosen to represent them. When the reparations have been paid we will all go back to our own villages and our own bands or clans or societies. There is no single man who is chief of this gathering. All are equal here."

"Yeah, but some are more equal than others. It's just natural for things t' be like that in any group of folks red or white. You, for instance, ain't likely to carry as much weight as, oh, say that gray-haired old fellow over there. I'm betting that in this bunch of grandfathers there has t' be one whose word is listened to closer than the others. Not like your father, maybe, but someone strong an' respected."

"Why do you ask this thing, Custis Long?"

Longarm grinned. "You see that fine-lookin' paint horse staked out over there?"

"Yes, of course. That is the best war horse of Yellow Wolf. It is a fine horse indeed."

"Yeah, but it's mine now."

Talking Bird's eyebrows shot up.

"I been playing Hand with some o' the fellows," Longarm said.

"Yes, I saw this."

"Well, now I come into possession of that paint pony. And I got no need for a war pony. Especially with this busted leg an' being on crutches like I am. So what I'd like t' do, you see, is to give my war pony to the big guy in camp."

115

Talking Bird's expression registered surprise. "You are a white man. I would think a man like you would return the pony to Yellow Wolf."

"If that's the right thing t' do I suppose I could, but that would be like saying I didn't value Yellow Wolf's wager. Like I didn't respect what he done when he put the horse up as his stake in the game. Leastways that's the way I was thinking of it. You tell me if I'm wrong about that, Talking Bird, because I don't know your ways in these things."

"You are correct, Custis Long. I just did not expect a white man to understand this."

"So will you point out t' me the best gent in the bunch I could give that horse to?"

Talking Bird paused for several moments in thought. Then he nodded. "Standing Tree is our most powerful shaman. It would be good for you to make your gift to him."

"Good enough," Longarm said. "Then would you please take me to meet Standing Tree?"

"Get the pony, Custis Long, and come with me. You can tell Standing Tree about this yourself. He has a little English." Talking Bird flashed a smile. "But please do not tell anyone else about this. He does not usually like for the white agents and commissioners to know that he understands their words when they speak among themselves."

Longarm laughed. "All right, friend. His secret is safe with me." Longarm pulled up the stake the paint was tied to—he really was a nice looking pony, with a broad, powerful chest and proud carriage—and led it along behind Talking Bird.

Chapter 25

Longarm stood with the other men, all of them including Longarm taking a final piss before going to bed. They hosed down the brush close to Standing Tree's lodge then the Kiowa pulled their breechclouts back in place while Longarm tucked his pecker back inside his britches and buttoned his fly. All together then, the seven Kiowa warriors and one white visitor trooped inside the tipi to their pallets.

The Indian men each had his own regular bed made of skins and soft furs. Longarm made do with some folded blankets that Standing Tree loaned him for the night. The buffalo skin lodge was large enough that eight occupants spread out on the floor did not seriously crowd it.

The Kiowas were all old men now but they once had been powerful warriors. As a shaman or medicine man Standing Tree might or might not have engaged in warfare himself. Longarm did not know and did not want to ask. And it made no difference now. The Kiowa accepted their surrender to the rule of law nowadays. The warpath was in the past for them. Now they were willing to take their reparation money and start down a new path leading to self-government.

The tribal leaders once were powerful but now their bellies sagged and their legs were bowed. When they stripped away their clothes for bed they looked like harmless old men. And old they were but not harmless. They still had the capacity for savagery. They had chosen to abandon war, and the entire white population of the southwest could be glad that they did.

Longarm laid his clothes aside as custom suggested, tucked his gunbelt under the blankets near the head of his bed and lay down. He could not help but smile when he saw that these old men retained the capacity for more than warfare. Some of them still retained other abilities too. Once the men were settled on their beds, three of them welcomed young women under the blankets with them.

The girls crept out of the shadows, dropped their dresses and slipped naked and nubile in bed with the old warriors.

This could become a rather noisy evening, Longarm thought as he pulled a blanket up to his chin and tried to settle down for the night. He heard some grunting and the slap of belly against belly and after a moment a man's voice calling out in the darkness.

The old buzzards could still get it up, Longarm thought with a smile. Good for them!

He felt a nudge on his shoulder and opened his eyes. A dark shape loomed over him.

Longarm felt no sense of danger however because the shape was that of a girl, slim and soft. And warm.

She was naked and her skin was very smooth and cool. He knew that because without waiting for an invitation she slipped beneath the blanket with him and lay snuggled against his side.

Her hand unerringly found his crotch, gently warming

his balls in her palm then lightly kneading his cock. It responded immediately, stretching and growing and turning as hard as marble.

The girl stroked and fondled him while she dipped her head to his body. Her lips were warm and her tongue moist. She suckled lightly on his nipple, the tip of her tongue teasing it and sending jolts of tingling sensation into his groin and balls as if there were a connection between them and the exquisitely sensitive nipple.

Longarm stroked the girl's body. Her back was smooth and her breasts firm and small. It was too dark inside the lodge for him to see her, but her flesh was young. Just how young he could only guess. There seemed to be at least a score of young women in the camp to take care of the needs—all of the needs—of the old men. The ages of the ones he had noticed ranged from the mid-twenties down into the early teens, he judged. This girl could be any one of them. In the dark he could not tell the difference.

Whoever she was, she was a delight beneath a blanket. Her tongue was in constant, teasing motion on his nipple while her hand continued to massage his cock and tickle his balls. She reached lower and ran the tip of one finger very softly around the rim of his asshole, then returned to his balls and again onto his shaft.

The combined effect of tongue and fingers aroused him to damn near a painful extent. His cock was throbbing and his hips responded with involuntary little thrusts in time with the rhythms of her tongue tip on Longarm's nipple.

He was oblivious to the sounds coming from the other beds inside the tipi but became conscious that a repeated low groan was issuing from his own throat.

If the girl kept this up, dammit, he was going to squirt all over himself.

The girl had a round, soft little ass. Longarm took a

handful of it and yanked her up on top of him. He thought he heard a muted giggle out of her. Pleased with herself for getting him so worked up, he guessed. Not that he minded. He was damn sure worked up and just about to burst.

She straddled him, reached down between their bodies and guided his aching pecker into the hot depths that he needed.

Her flesh closed wetly around him, and she gasped a little as its length penetrated deep inside her slender body.

Longarm took hold of her tits. They were hard and small. He squeezed, and the girl began to move her hips in slow circles.

She seemed willing to continue that indefinitely. He was not.

He felt the surge of heat in his balls and he flung himself upward, driving hard into her.

The girl cried out aloud as Longarm came. His seed spewed out in jets of liquid heat, and he shuddered at the power of his climax.

He did not realize until it was over how powerful it had been. Or that in the passion of it he must have hurt her. His grip on her breasts had contracted with all his strength. He must have damn near ripped them off, but she did not pull away. That must have been what made her cry out though. Realizing, he quickly loosened his hold on her and tried to massage her tits instead.

The girl lay flat against his chest, her hands lightly running over his shoulders and throat and face while again her lips found Longarm's nipple and began to lick and to suck the tiny bud of pleasure there.

Longarm was still inside her and he felt once again the stir of deep arousal.

But this time, he told himself, he would take his time about it.

The girl knew what she was doing, and she did it mighty

well. Longarm relaxed and let her take charge of this very pleasant coupling while all around the aging Kiowa warriors did the same with their nubile young bed partners.

Soon Longarm felt himself thrusting and grunting in time with the girl's exertions and soon after that all conscious thought was wiped away by the power of raw animal urges.

He cried out, his voice a thin imitation of a war cry, as again he came.

Kiowa hospitality, he considered, was more than just a little pleasant.

Chapter 26

"Are you all right? I worried about you when you didn't come back last night," Jimmy told him. Jimmy was busy removing the harness from the buggy horse. He hung the harness on a peg in the wall of the long cavalry stable and picked up a curry comb.

"I'm fine," Longarm assured him. "Wanta know what I found out?"

"Of course."

"I know why the Dekins gang is coming here. What I don't know is who they're supposed t' meet or what that has to do with anything. But I know what their purpose is."

Jimmy tilted his head and looked at the little horse's feet. "I don't think I can clean his feet with just this one hand, and you aren't steady enough to be messing with his feet while you're still on crutches."

"Leave them be for now. It's all right."

"So what about the Dekins boys?" Jimmy asked, dropping the curry comb into a bucket and fetching out a dandybrush to use next.

"Gold," Longarm said. "They're coming here to rob a mess of gold."

"Where would they find gold around here?"

Longarm told him, adding, "Though I'm damned if I know how they intend t' get it. There must be upwards of seventy, eighty men in the delegation that's supposed to receive the reparation money. You wouldn't think a bunch of robbers would think they could take on that many Kiowa warriors all at once. And the army is sure to be sending a guard detail with the gold. The Dekinses have to be smarter than to take on the whole damn U.S. Army."

"Which may be why they are meeting someone here."

"It can't be one of the Indians themselves. There is nothing the Dekins boys could give a Kiowa that would make it worthwhile for him to help them rob his own people, so I reckon we can rule all o' them out. But it could be Sgt. Johnson or one of his people here at Fort Larned. Or it might could be someone in the guard detail. A white man might be found who would betray his outfit in exchange for a heavy enough poke of gold coin," Longarm said. He pulled out a cheroot and lighted it, never mind that they were inside a barn where smoking was generally not allowed. The building was made of sandstone, and the floor was clean of straw or other combustibles.

"What worried me more than anything else isn't the gold anyway," he went on while Jimmy finished grooming the horse.

"You don't care about the gold?" Jimmy asked over his shoulder. He was finished with the dandybrush and was combing out the horse's forelock.

"Oh, I care about it. Sure I do. But the government has plenty of money. If it happens to lose some to a robbery it'd be a shame but not a disaster. What'd be much worse, Jimmy, is if those Kiowa don't get what they been promised. Talking Bird let me know clear enough that the tribe has young men down there who haven't had a chance to prove themselves in battle and older men who hate the notion that they got whipped by the white man's army. Another broken promise, never mind that it wouldn't be the government's fault if the gold is stolen before it can be delivered, and those young Kiowa could break out of the reservation and go on a rampage through half of Texas and all through the Nations. They could terrorize people across ten thousand square miles of country and be a bitch to run down and reel in again."

Jimmy whistled. "I see what you mean. The prospect of another Indian war is scary."

"We got to make sure it doesn't happen," Longarm said. "Come hell or high water. Did you hear or see anything yesterday that might give us an idea who the turncoat would be?"

"No. But . . ." He paused, then shrugged and looked away without continuing.

"What?" Longarm prodded.

"It isn't anything."

"You're probably right. But go ahead an' tell me anyway. Just in case."

"I did see one of the soldiers sneaking around behind the storeroom. Johnson took two of the men over to Officer's Row to do some maintenance work there. This private was hiding around the corner, watching. When Johnson and his detail got out of sight, this man ducked low and hurried around to the back of the old commissary building. I lost sight of him then and didn't see where he went or what he did, but he brought attention to himself by the sneaky way he was walking. To tell you the truth, Longarm, I wouldn't have paid any attention to him if he had not been acting so suspiciously."

"Whoever the Dekins brothers intend to meet here would not necessarily be accustomed to larceny," Longarm said. "An accomplished thief would know better than to call attention to himself that way. Dekins' contact might be an amateur. But a willing one if the payoff is big enough."

"How much money are we talking about?" Jimmy asked.

"I don't know. Talking Bird didn't say, an' I didn't ask. I didn't want to be too curious about the money. After all, I never told the Kiowa that I'm a deputy marshal. An' if things go wrong and you and me can't stop this robbery from happening, I don't want the whole Kiowa nation looking back at this nosy white man and thinking maybe I had something t' do with it."

"Do you really think there will be a war if the money is stolen?"

Longarm shrugged. "I can't say that for sure either way, kid, but one thing I do know for certain sure and that is that the possibility exists. It *could* happen. Far as I'm concerned, that is more than enough cause for worry."

"I've read about Indian warfare. It sounds ugly."

"Believe me, Jim, it is. I've seen some of it my own self. Seen the bodies of children that 've been scalped and mutilated. Women with their tits cut off and their bellies slit open to get at babies that weren't born yet. Men stripped naked and staked out spread-eagle then fires built in their crotches. An' all of this done while the people was still alive. Don't never let anybody tell you, Jimmy, that the Indians was wronged and never at fault for any of the shit that went on out here in the wild old days. Me, I respect Indians and their ways. I figure they're entitled to be let be. But I got no illusions about Lo, the Poor Indian. He can be one murdering son of a bitch, clever as a fox and mean as a snake. That's something you want t' keep in mind."

"Do you really think we can stop the gang, Longarm?"

Longarm grinned. "Hell yes, son. Not only *can* we stop them, we are damn well *going* to. Believe it."

Jimmy laughed. "All three-fourths of us."

"That's right, kid. Us two cripples are gonna rain hell down on Bob an' Brad Dekins. Count on it."

Chapter 27

"Where the hell you been?" Johnson demanded when Longarm and Jimmy went in for lunch. "You wasn't here last night or again this morning."

"I was what you might call . . . visiting," Longarm said with a wink.

"Getting some of that red pussy?" Johnson laughed. "So that's why you bought all that t'bacca. Mister, you didn't need anywhere near that much. Those Injuns would sell their women for a handful of spit. Women don't mean nothing to them. They got no human feelings. I know. I fought them many a time. Killed me a bunch of them too."

"Is that a fact."

"Damn right it is. I served under Gen'rul Crook till I got too stove up to walk very far. Would've been with him still if my feet hadn't give out."

"I've heard about Crook. Isn't he down in Arizona Territory now?"

"He sure is, and I wisht I was with him down there chasing those Apaches just like we done with Sitting Bull. We run him down, you know. Whipped his ass good."

Longarm nodded. "You men have done good work. The papers back east all say that. You soldiers make us proud."

The grizzled old sergeant beamed. "Damn right."

Later, when they were alone after lunch though, Longarm told Jimmy, "Johnson is full of shit. He was infantry."

"Crook doesn't have infantry?"

"Oh, sure he does. An' Johnson may well've been one of those soldiers that the Indians call walks-a-heap. But nobody whipped Sitting Bull's butt. I've met Sitting Bull and that is one smart Indian. He slipped away to Canada where our army can't get to him. If he comes back down to the States it will be in his own good time."

"You know Sitting Bull?"

Longarm shook his head. "I don't claim to know him. Hell, I doubt that any white man can honestly say he knows the man. But I've met him. I've seen the kind of leader he is, and he is one formidable opponent."

"What about the Apaches?"

"Tough. Damn tough. And vicious. Not as smart as Sitting Bull, I think, and not so many of them as there are Lakota which is a mighty good thing because they're fighters. Maybe more so than any other tribe. The army has its hands full when it goes to trying to run them down and bring them in."

"And the Indians that are here now?"

"Kiowa. They're born fighters too. They give no quarter and they ask none. You don't wanta get crossways with any of them. Not to change the subject, kid, but which one of the soldiers in there at lunch is the one you saw sneaking around behind Johnson's back yesterday?"

"He was seated on the right side of the table, second man from the end. The end toward the kitchen, I mean. I heard someone call him Dawson."

Longarm nodded. "I remember him. Kinda red-headed? Before he got gray?"

"That's the one."

"I think maybe we should keep an eye on Pvt. Dawson, Jim."

"I'll do it. I can get around a lot quicker than you. What are you going to do?"

Longarm grinned. "First thing," he said, "is get a little rest. I didn't get hardly a wink o' sleep last night."

"With all those wild Indians around, I don't blame you," Jimmy said solemnly. "You must have been awfully worried they would try to kill you."

Longarm laughed, thinking about the girl who had shared his bed for the night. And who was the reason he had been just too busy to think much about sleep. "You got a lot t' learn, kid."

"Now what?"

Longarm laughed again, loud and long.

Jimmy spent the afternoon spying on Pvt. Dawson while Longarm stumped over to the post headquarters where he talked Sgt. Johnson and Boston—it turned out the man was from Boston; his name was Polish and sounded like someone clearing their throat—into a friendly game of poker.

During the course of the game, which he made sure he was losing, he slipped a few questions into the sparse flow of observations, comments and complaints.

"What are those redskins doing over there anyway?"

"Shit, you think they tell us anything? The fucking army, I mean. Them Injuns can't speak a word of white man's lingo so they couldn't say anything if they wanted to."

"And the army hasn't said?"

"No. Like I said, man, they don't tell us nothing. Twice

131

a year they send out supplies. Enough for a full infantry company. That's why we got stuff to spare for you travelers that come by. An' they get around to paying us every two or three months. That's about it."

"That and moving personnel in or out," Boston put in. "We got two new guys just last year."

"What about mail?" Longarm asked. "Surely you get mail here."

"We get it but not here. Nearest town is twenty-some miles. We get our mail there."

"Spend it there too," Boston said.

"How do you get there? I haven't seen any horses."

"Wagon. We got a wagon and team assigned here."

"How's come . . . ?"

"You ain't seen it because it ain't here right now," Johnson said. "We got eight men assigned, plus me and the cook. We take turn-about going into town. Right now it's Hankins' and Joyner's turn. They'll be back in a couple days, then it'll be somebody else's turn."

"Mine," Boston said firmly. "I go next. Me and Dawson. Don't you go forgetting that, Johnson."

"Bite my ass, Boston. I know how to make out a duty roster as good as any of you. You'll get your turn."

"So you don't know why those Indians are here?" Longarm asked.

Johnson shrugged. "Picking yarbs and mushrooms or something. Hell, why does a Injun do anything. They aren't like white men. They don't have no purpose or anything. And they're a bunch of old fucks, most of them."

"Except the women," Boston said. "They got some young women with them. Good-looking bitches, some of them." He reached down and cupped his balls and grinned when he said it.

"Injuns got no pride," Johnson explained. "They use

132

their women to get stuff." He flashed a smile. "Not that we're complaining, mind you. It's handy having some pussy close by, and to tell you the honest truth, Long, some of those Injun gals are better than what we get in town. I don't know why they're here, but we don't mind having them around, I can tell you that."

Longarm grunted and looked at his cards. The deck was old and too long used and if he had been so inclined he could have learned to read the backs as easily as the fronts. He could have cleaned the soldiers out. Certainly they could have cleaned him out if they wanted. They obviously regarded the game as a means of passing time, not raking in money.

He could understand that easily enough. But surely someone here had to know about the reparation money and the Dekins bunch. Otherwise why would the gang be coming here with the expectation of meeting someone?

It was puzzling, Longarm thought. Unless this whole thing was merely a blind alley, another false trail laid down by the Dekins boys to throw Carl and Dutch off the scent.

It just could be that he and Jimmy Wheelock were completely wasting their time coming down here. If so then Longarm sure as hell hoped the other boys were able to catch up to the Dekins brothers. Longarm wanted those sons of bitches taken down. Hard.

Chapter 28

"Learn anything this afternoon?" Longarm asked Jimmy the Kid after supper.

"Not about Dawson, but I just now saw some Indians out there with meat to trade. And, uh, there were some women with them too. I asked Pvt. Worden. He said the girls will be out back of the laundry building tonight for anybody that wants them."

"You want to go join the soldiers for a taste of red meat?"

Jimmy nodded. "If you don't mind."

"Me? Hell no. No reason I should object t' you getting a little ass."

"Are you coming?"

Longarm shook his head. "I don't think so." He stopped short of telling Jimmy that he'd already had his share. He did wonder, though, if he would be able to spot the girl if he saw her again. It had been dark in that tipi, and all he ever saw of her were silhouettes and shadows. Inwardly he couldn't help but laugh a little. He had to admit to a wee small niggle of worry; if he saw the girl and recognized her it could turn out that she was butt-ugly, and wouldn't that ruin the memories he had of her.

"Could I . . ." Jimmy hesitated, then asked, "Could I ask a really big favor of you?"

"You can ask. Remains t' be seen whether I'll do whatever it is that you're wanting."

"It's about my bandages. They're all soiled with food and snot and filth. I was wondering would you change them for me before I go over to the laundry."

"Sure, Jim, I'll do that for you."

They went to their quarters, Jimmy matching his pace to Longarm's painfully slow progress on the crutches. Jimmy pulled a stool over to the side of Longarm's bunk so Longarm could sit and concentrate on what he was doing instead of teetering on the sticks.

"I want to ask you something," Jimmy said when Longarm began unwinding the wrappings.

"Sure."

"I want you to be honest with me. How . . . how bad is it?"

"We'll know in a minute. Uh . . . there." Longarm dropped the last of the soiled linen onto the floor and stared at what was left of James Wheelock's face. The kid had been handsome. Once.

"Well?"

Longarm paused. He wanted to tell Jimmy the truth. But . . . shit! "It's too soon t' tell for sure. You got a whole lot o' healing to go."

"I know that, but how bad is it?"

"Straight out? It's bad, Jim. I've seen worse, mind you, but this is bad." He squinted and tilted his head first one way and then the other while he looked at what was there. "Mostly it's the eye," he said finally. "That empty socket looks like hell. You'll want t' get you a patch to cover that. That'll help a lot."

"All right. What else?"

Longarm peered at the damage again, then said, "There's still some swelling. Still a lot o' healing yet to come. For now . . . Jimmy, the truth is you look like you was assaulted by a bunch o' knee-walking drunks having themselves a quilting bee an' trying to piece together a face outa spare parts."

"You aren't very encouraging."

"Kid, if you don't want the truth then don't be asking me for it. I'm only tryin' to do what you said."

"I know, but I . . . oh, shit."

"Look, it's gonna heal plenty from what it's like now. You got to give it time."

"And keep my bandages, is that it?"

"Yeah, Jimmy, I'd say that's pretty much it."

"Thanks. I suppose."

"Hold still," Longarm said, "while I put this fresh wrap on you. It won't be as neat a job as that doc did, but I'll do the best I can." He smiled a little. "At least you got a good start on growing a beard now, and beards are distinguished. Or so they tell me."

"Fuck," Jimmy grumbled.

"The good thing," Longarm said while he continued to wind linen around and around Jimmy's head, "is that the part of you that counts ain't been touched. A man's worth don't have anything t' do with what he looks like. It's his heart and his gut an' his brain that really matters. You still got those, kid."

"I told you not to call me that any more," Jimmy snapped.

"Sorry. I keep forgetting."

137

Longarm finished the bandaging in silence, then reached for a cheroot while Jimmy hurried out into the new-fallen night in search of a woman's body to give him comfort and release.

Life, Longarm reminded himself, is not an exercise in fairness. Not hardly.

Chapter 29

Longarm was pacing the floor—or as close to it as he could come on crutches—when Jimmy returned to their quarters that night.

"That miserable little bitch," Jimmy announced as he came in the door.

"Something wrong?"

"Yes, there is something wrong. The little slut wouldn't take it in the mouth. All she wanted was a straight fuck. That isn't what I was paying for."

"I reckon she didn't know that," Longarm said.

"The bitch," Jimmy repeated.

"So maybe you can get yourself a blow job from one o' the white whores in town tomorrow. At least they'll speak English. You can work it out before you pay anything."

That got the kid's attention. "We're going to town?"

"Yeah. First thing after breakfast. It occurred t' me while I was waiting here for you that sometimes I can be as dumb as anybody. The soldier boys here don't seem t' know anything about any reparation money, and there's too many Kiowa in that camp down there to be handled by the Dekins bunch. So what does that tell you?"

"You said earlier it was maybe a false trail," Jimmy reminded him.

"Yeah, I did say that, but we're talking about gold here. An' the Dekins brothers. I believe what the fella told the little whore you had up north. They're coming here t' meet a fellow and t' pull a job. Except there's nothing says they have t' hit that shipment here at Larned. I'm thinking they plan to rob the gold before it ever gets here.

"So what me and you got to find out, Jimmy, is exactly where and when the gold is s'posed to arrive."

"Do you think we can learn that in this town you mentioned?"

"If they got a telegraph station we can. I figure we'll wire Billy Vail. Get him to contact whoever the hell in Washington would be in charge of such. He can wire us back with the information, and we'll make sure t' be there waiting when the gold arrives."

Jimmy nodded. "All right. Tomorrow then."

They were up at first light. Jimmy hitched the buggy, then joined Longarm in the enlisted men's dining hall where Longarm got directions to the town Sgt. Johnson mentioned the previous afternoon.

"You're moving on?"

"We might could be back. It depends on what way we decide t' go from here. If we're passing by again we'll likely come this way."

"Yeah, well, I ain't giving no refunds on what you paid for room and board."

"We aren't asking for any."

"That's fine then. Come again if you want."

As soon as breakfast was over Jimmy loaded their gear into the buggy and then set off in the direction Johnson indicated. Late in the morning they passed a freight wagon pulled by a team of heavy cobs. There were two uniformed soldiers on the driving box. The bed was half full of small kegs and bundles. The wagon passed without so much as a nod of greeting.

"Who was that?" Jimmy asked.

"Couple guys coming back from a pass," Longarm explained, filling the kid in on the off duty rotation.

"Surly sons of bitches."

Longarm grinned. "Prob'ly so wore out from a week of hard fucking that they didn't hardly see the two of us."

Jimmy grunted, then said, "Lucky sons of bitches."

"Make up your mind," Longarm said with a chuckle.

They reached town in mid-afternoon. A set of gleaming rails showed why the place had grown up here instead of out by the army post where it must originally have been located.

"Good," Longarm said. "There's a telegraph station. Tell you what, kid, whyn't you drop me off at the depot, then you can go over to the hotel yonder and get us checked in. But no government vouchers for payment, mind. I still don't wanta advertise who we are."

"All right. You want me to come pick you up when I'm done?"

"No, just put the rig up and see to the horse. I can make it over there on my own. It ain't all that far."

"Whatever you say."

Longarm lowered himself carefully to the ground outside the train depot and went inside. The telegrapher was a young, earnest-looking fellow.

"I hope you can keep a confidence," Longarm told him before he picked up a pencil and began composing the message for the boss back in Denver.

"I can't tell you if I can or not, mister, because that's a secret and I don't tell those out of school."

Longarm smiled. And wrote out the message. He was in the process of paying for it when he heard the roar of gunfire somewhere nearby.

"Shit," he mumbled, grabbing for his crutches and hurrying out as rapidly as he could go.

Longarm's first thought was of the Dekins gang, but it wasn't. The commotion was caused by some cowboys— four, no five of them—riding hell-for-leather down the main street with their pistols blazing.

Kids, dogs and women scattered before them. Horses spooked and broke their reins at the tie rails to thunder off ahead of the stampeding cowboys.

Longarm was already in the street, his Colt in hand, before he realized there was no real danger. The reckless young men were shooting in the air or at store signs, not at people.

As the group neared, hoofs flashing and revolvers booming, Longarm tried to duck back onto the sidewalk. The tip of his left crutch slipped in a bit of muddy horse piss on the ground, and his right crutch was only loosely tucked into his armpit so he could handle the .44. Off balance and with no help support from the broken leg, he fell, landing on his side heavily enough to knock the wind out of him.

The cowboys saw and with yips and war whoops swerved out away from him.

Down the block, though, Longarm could see Jimmy the Kid race into the street. He took a wide-legged stance squarely in front of the racing cowboys and brought the twin tubes of his sawed-off shotgun up.

Jimmy's expression was grim. The set of his body showed that the cowboys could ride him down but they could not make him flinch.

People were fixing to die here. And all the cowboys

were doing was a little hoorahing on their way into town for a drink and maybe a woman.

"Kid. Don't shoot!" Longarm screamed. He struggled to get his crutches under him, cussed and shoved the Colt back into his holster and tried again, coming tottering upright.

Jimmy saw and yanked the muzzles of his shotgun toward the sky. His finger must have reflexively closed because one barrel roared, the heavy load of shot flying harmless into the air.

It was the turn of the cowboys' horses to be spooked with the noise and flame in front of them. Two of them reared, nearly unseating their riders, and all of them veered over to the other side of the street.

"Watch out, dammit," one of the young men shouted while others cursed. "You could hurt somebody."

Jimmy watched them disappear around a street corner, then turned and ran to Longarm.

"Are you hurt? I saw you go down and I thought it was the Dekins bunch. I thought they shot you."

"I'm fine. Damn crutch slipped, that's all. Jimmy?"

"Yes?"

"You got two shots in that thing."

"That's right."

"You was gonna stand right there an' take as many of them with you as you could before you went down yourself."

When Jimmy did not respond, Longarm added, "Weren't you gonna do that? Weren't you?"

Jimmy shrugged.

Longarm brushed some of the dust and street dirt from his clothing while he thought for a moment. "You got more t' live for than you seem to think, Jim. Don't go doin' stupid stuff that will get you killed."

"You think I was interested in suicide?"

"I think you came damn close. Don't you be doing any-

143

thing like that, Jim." Longarm smiled. "If for nothing else, Jimmy, keep in mind that we're partners. And I'm needin' your help to bring those bastards down."

"Not that it is any of your business, Custis Long, but I will promise not to kill myself. At least not until this job is finished."

Longarm peered at Jimmy but the kid's expression, whatever it might be, was hidden beneath those layers of linen bandage.

"Settle for that, Longarm. It is all I can give you."

After a moment Longarm nodded. "All right, kid. That's fair enough. Now tell me, do we have a room yet? I'm feeling kinda tired of a sudden."

Chapter 30

The hotel rooms were all on the second floor and Longarm did not want to be going up and down the stairs any more than was necessary. He led Jimmy the Kid to a pair of comfortable armchairs in the hotel lobby and settled onto one, Jimmy first laying Longarm's crutches aside for him then taking a seat in the chair beside Longarm's.

"What I'll do, kid, is t' set in the lobby here an' catch up with whatever newspapers they got on hand. After supper you can help me up them steps just the one time, an' I can stay there until we come down for breakfast tomorrow. That won't be so awful bad, I reckon. Meantime you can come an' go however you please."

Longarm winked at him. "If you ask at that saloon across the street I expect you can find out where a man can get himself a blow job in this town."

"Do you want me to bring a woman back to the room for you?" Jimmy offered.

"That's damn nice o' you, but I expect I can get along tonight without one."

145

"Let me know if you change your mind." Jimmy chuckled and added, "I have a question if you don't mind."

"Go right ahead."

The chuckle turned into a laugh. "It's about our expense reimbursement when we get back to Denver."

"Fine. What about it?"

"Can we put the cost of whores on the voucher?"

Longarm grinned. "Jimmy, I like the way you think. An' the truth is, I expect you really can get paid back for any you go to . . . an' pay . . . for information. Like that little old gal back up the way where you found out about the gang coming to Fort Larned. I'd think we could be reimbursed for that. It's legitimate. But, uh, maybe not for whatever you spend this evening."

"I was just joking but you're serious, aren't you?"

"Hell, why not. O' course Henry might change things on the official paperwork. Pretty things up for what he turns in so it don't actually come right out an' say. Write it down as buying information, not pussy, if you see what I mean."

"My oh my, I am really going to miss this," Jimmy said with a sigh.

"Miss what, Jim?"

"I'm going to miss being a deputy."

"What makes you think . . ."

"Now who's joking," Jimmy interrupted. "You're just trying to make me feel better. But the truth is, you know . . . and I know . . . that as soon as we get back to Denver and Marshal Vail sees what happened to me, my days of being a deputy U.S. marshal are over."

"Does it mean that much to you?"

Jimmy turned toward Longarm, his one eye glistening bright inside the hole in the bandages. "Yes," he said. "It means . . . meant . . . that much to me. I might not have

146

shown it, but all my life the most important thing I could think of was to be a peace officer. Getting this appointment was a dream come true. Now look. That bomb turned me into half a man. One hand. One eye. Shit, Longarm, just look." Jimmy stood and started toward the door, but Longarm called him back.

"Set yourself down an' keep that blind snake inside your britches a minute longer, Jimmy."

"All right. Why?"

"I got an idea. An' a confession if you don't mind."

"A confession? You?"

"That's right, Jim. A confession of sorts. When we first was put together, you and me and the other boys sent after the Dekinses, I had some doubts about you. You came across awful cocky."

"I was scared," Jimmy whispered. "Scared I wouldn't measure up. You and Dutch, Longarm, you are my heroes. My idols. You in particular. I'd heard so much about you. And I . . . I guess I wanted so badly to fit in that I tried too hard or something. I'm sorry."

"No, Jim, I'm the one should be sorry here. I judged you mighty harsh, but you more than measure up. You got sand in your belly, Jimmy. I'm proud t' ride with you. I want you t' know that. I'd partner with you any time."

"Never again though," Jimmy said, a hint of bitterness creeping into his tone of voice.

"Look, I'm speaking out of school here. Premature like. But it's true you won't be able t' stay on as a deputy. When we get back, Billy Vail won't have no choice about that."

"I know it. I don't blame him. Or you. I know how it is."

"The thing is, kid, there's more ways to enforce the law than just as a deputy marshal."

"What do you mean, Longarm?"

"I mean I can't be making promises for somebody else. But it happens that I have a right good friend who works for a private detective agency."

"A Pink?" Jimmy asked.

"No, he's not with the Pinkertons. Personally I don't have much use for them. The Pinks sometimes get the idea that they're above the law. My friend works for Rocky Mountain."

"I've heard of them. They work with the railroads a lot, don't they?"

"That an' guarding shipments o' gold an' silver out o' the mines. They act as guards. Investigate thefts an' embezzlement, things like that too. I got a lot of respect for them. An' as smart as you are, I think you could fit in with them. Even with one eye an' missing most of that hand. I think you got what it takes, kid. When we get back I'll see if my friend can do you any good there."

"It would be quite a come-down from being a deputy marshal though, Longarm."

"Jim, let me tell you something. You've rode as a deputy. All the rest of your life you'll have that, knowing that you've rode with the best. An' it ain't myself that I'm wanting to hold high when I say that, Jimmy. You've rode in mighty good company. You've worn that badge an' acquitted yourself right proud. No one can ever take that away from you, no matter where you go from here."

"I never looked at it that way."

"From here, Jim, you can either think on this time with pride or you can choose t' feel sorry for yourself. I know what I hope you'll do. But the choice is gonna be yours."

"Out there in the street today . . ." Jimmy said haltingly, then stopped.

"I know, Jim. You don't have t' explain."

"I wanted . . . when I thought those cowboys were the

Dekins gang . . . I wanted them to kill me. I wanted to kill them too. But I didn't really want to survive a second encounter with them."

"Don't be doing any o' that shit again, Jim. You make a good partner. An' it really pisses me off when I go an' let a partner of mine get hisself killed."

"I wouldn't want to piss you off," Jimmy said with a small laugh.

"Good. Now go on an' have yourself some fun. I'll be fine right here with my newspapers to read an' people to watch coming in an' out."

"I can come back and help you up the stairs later."

"Don't worry about it. I can get the bellboy t' give me a hand when I decide t' go up to the room. What number did you say we're in?"

Jimmy gave him the room key. "If you are sure. . . ."

Longarm laughed. "Go on, Jim. Get yourself that blow job. Hell, get two of them while you're at it. Take two girls at once. That's another experience you won't easy forget."

"Two at the same time? Oh, my."

"Go on now. You're interfering with my reading."

"Don't wait up for me," Jimmy said on his way out the door.

149

Chapter 31

Longarm froze in place. He felt like his blood had frozen in his veins. Standing over at the hotel desk collecting her key was a young, pale, very pretty woman with brown hair done up in ringlets. She wore an attractive and somewhat understated dress, rather fetching little wisp of a hat with a veil attached to it and was carrying a parasol.

There was no handbag to match the parasol, and Longarm knew why. The handbag that used to go so nicely with the parasol had blown up one day back in Arnpelt, Kansas.

There was no question in Longarm's mind that this was the same girl who delivered the bomb that let the Dekins bunch escape that day. Delivered the bomb and then promptly disappeared. She was a part of the gang or as good as.

And she was here. In this hotel. Close to where the Dekins boys were supposed to be planning their next job.

Longarm sat very still, peering over the top of the newspaper he'd been reading. He watched while the girl received her key and then went lightly up the stairs that led to the rooms. She seemed to be alone. But then appearances matter little. He certainly had reason to know that about this particular girl. She might look like a lady but she damn sure was not one.

He waited until she was gone, then collected his crutches and made his way laboriously across the lobby to the desk.

"Yes, sir, how may I help you?" the clerk asked.

"I was wondering if you got any more newspapers."

"I believe we might have although they would be out of date."

"Oh, that's all right. I been out o' touch for a spell. I'm enjoying catchin' up on what's been going on."

"I shall be glad to bring you whatever I can find, sir."

"Thanks. Say, a minute ago I noticed a girl standin' here."

"Yes, sir?"

"I only caught a glimpse of her, but I got t' ask. Was that Miss Adele Feinbaum from Detroit, Michigan?"

"No, sir, she is not."

"Pity," Longarm said with a leer and a wink. "I, uh, suppose she's with her husband then?"

The desk clerk's expression turned cold. "The young lady is traveling alone. She expects to meet her fiancé here. I doubt she would appreciate having her privacy disturbed."

"Sorry. An' don't you worry none about me approachin' the lady. I wouldn't think of it. Not with her being promised an' everything."

"Very well, sir. Now if you will excuse me, I shall look for those newspapers you wanted."

"Yes. Thanks."

Longarm took the opportunity while he was already up to find the water closet and take a leak, then went back to the chair where he'd been parked for most of the afternoon. He expected to be there for quite a while longer while he waited to see if anyone named Dekins wandered past or any of the boys who rode with Brad and little brother Bob, the few of them that he had some idea what they looked like. Thank goodness for artist sketches on wanted posters.

"There's good new, Jim," Longarm said when a rather disheveled—but very relaxed—Jimmy Wheelock finally returned to the hotel that night.

"Good. Tell me about it."

"Upstairs where we got some privacy," Longarm responded.

"All right, if you think so." Jimmy collected Longarm's crutches and helped Longarm up the stairs to their room. "I have to say, Longarm, that your news cannot be much better than mine."

"How's that, Jimmy?"

"I am very pleased to tell you that the women here are much more accommodating than the Kiowa girls were. At least when it comes to, um, certain activities."

Longarm smiled. Apparently the kid was able to get that blow job he'd been wanting so badly.

When they were inside and the door closed behind them Jimmy asked, "Now what is this news of yours?"

"The girl," Longarm said.

"Girl? Which girl?"

"Bradley Dekins' accomplice, that's the girl I mean. You remember her, don't you?"

"For the rest of my life I will remember that bitch," Jimmy retorted. "I see her every day, everywhere I look. If I am lucky someday I may see her in the flesh again too."

"Then I'd have t' say you are mighty lucky, Jim."

"You can't mean. . . ."

Longarm nodded. "Right here, Jimmy. In this hotel. Right down the hall, in fact."

"What room number?"

"I don't know, Jim, and I don't want t' call any more attention to us by asking."

"Aren't you going to arrest her?"

"Hell yes, we will. But not yet. We don't want to tip our hand before the rest o' the gang shows up an' we can get a handle on how they intend to rob that gold."

"She could get away," Jimmy protested.

"The way I see it, Jim, you are gonna make real sure that she doesn't. I figure you got plenty o' reason to see her rot in prison."

"Rot in a grave is more like it," Jimmy said. "I'd like to see that woman dead."

"We don't go around killin' women . . . nor anybody else for that matter . . . as a personal vengeance sort o' thing," Longarm reminded him. "You are a deputy U.S. marshal an' I expect you to act like it."

"I could walk down the hall and kill her right this minute." He touched the grip of the shotgun that always dangled at his side these days. "It's tempting," Jimmy admitted.

"There ain't no sin in the temptation, just when you give in to it."

"Even so. . . ."

"You're a good deputy, Jim. I know you're gonna do what's right."

"Then you know more than I do about me."

"Come on, Jimmy. Let's get some sleep. Tomorrow might could be a real busy day."

Jimmy turned to stare at the door. He stood there for

what seemed a very long time, long enough that Longarm began to worry that he really would go find the woman and murder her. But after a bit Jimmy sniffed loudly, then turned away and began unbuttoning his shirt.

Chapter 32

"No, I won't do it."

"The hell you won't," Longarm snapped back at him. "You may not like it. I don't blame you for that. But you damn well got t' do it. Get that through your head. You're gonna hole up right here in this hotel room an' not show your face . . . okay, in your case not show your bandages . . . until I tell you otherwise.

"We know the word got around about there being a pair of blown up deputies. We run into that up north, remember? The gang is sure t' know what they did to us, and if we're both seen on the street they're likely t' hear and make the connection.

"One man with a broke leg can be anybody. Fellas come off horses ever day an' get busted up, so it ain't nothing to see a man on crutches with his leg in a splint. But you, you're in a different situation with your face all wrapped up. No, Jimmy, you got to hole up here until we get a handle on this bunch. Then I'll be needin' you to take them down. I got to have your help for that an' anyway you're entitled to be in on it. God knows you've paid the price of admission."

"I can't just stay here," Jimmy wailed.

"O' course you can. You got excuse enough. The hotel people will think you're hurting from your injuries. Anybody asks, I'll say you was in a fire . . . we shoulda thought about that before . . . and I fell and got hurt trying to rescue your sorry ass." Longarm grinned. "Might as well make myself into a hero if we're gonna spin a yarn.

"Seriously though, you don't need no excuses. Your bandages are excise enough for you t' lay low. I'll just have your meals carried up to you. An' I'll get them t' bring in one of those chairs with the bowl built under the seat so's you don't have to squat over a thunder mug. And I'll send up some magazines an' newspapers for you t' read."

"I don't want to sit here and read. I want . . ."

"You want to go kill the sons of bitches that done this to you. I know that, Jim, an' I won't try and take that away from you. Comes the time, you'll be in on it. That's a promise."

"What will you be doing?" Jimmy's voice remained sullen but he seemed to have accepted Longarm's argument.

"One thing I ain't going to be doing is running up an' down these steps. Not on these crutches, I ain't. I'm apt to fall an' kill myself if I try that. Damn things are slippery, and I don't trust 'em all that much. So once I get down there I'm gonna stay there. I'll have something to eat, then I'll go see if Billy sent an answer to my telegram about when an' how that gold is supposed to arrive.

"Once we know that, we can make a plan about how to intercept those bastards an' take them down."

Jimmy nodded. His body posture, shoulders stiff and fist clenched, suggested he was still pissed off. But he said, "All right. If you say so."

"I wouldn't say it, Jimmy, if I didn't think it was necessary. Now you an' that shotgun get yourselves ready. I'm gonna go down and have me some breakfast before I make my way over to the depot. I'll send something up for you."

"Shit!" was Jimmy's only comment.

Breakfast lay warm and comfortable in his belly as Longarm slowly swung along on his crutches. He kind of hated to admit it but he was starting to get used to the damn things. At least they were not as miserably uncomfortable as they had been to begin with.

Stairs still bothered him. But he'd learned to cheat by setting the broken leg lightly down to help his balance while he brought his left leg up to the next step. That made it easier.

Now he mounted the few steps to the railroad platform and thumped his way inside the tiny ticket office.

"Good mornin'. Did you receive the reply to my message yet?" he asked the Kansas and Pacific telegrapher.

"Not since I've been on this morning but it might have come in overnight. Let me look." The fellow rummaged through several message slips in a wooden tray and straightened with a smile. "Yes, sir. Here 'tis." He handed Longarm an envelope.

"Thanks." Longarm took the yellow form over to one of the waiting area benches and sat, laying his crutches aside before he opened the envelope.

He scanned Billy Vail's response, then grunted softly to himself, his forehead furrowed in concentration.

Knowing when and how the gold was being shipped was the lesser part of his problem. Knowing what the Dekins gang intended was the much greater problem. And he could only guess at that.

Unless. . . .

Chapter 33

Longarm clumped his way back to the hotel as rapidly as the crutches could get him there. This, he figured, would be Jimmy's big moment. The kid wanted to get back at the girl who was running with the Dekins boys. Fine.

Longarm intended to take her into custody and let Jimmy do the interrogating afterward. If the girl weren't scared near out of her mind by that prospect she certainly ought to be.

It shouldn't take long to break her, he believed. As soon as she peached on the boys Longarm would tug on Jimmy's chain and call off any rough stuff. No problem.

There was no one behind the desk at the hotel. The only other person in the lobby was a businessman who was loudly, and repeatedly, thumping the bell that was supposed to summon the clerk or the bell boy, neither of whom seemed to be available at the moment.

"Oh, shit," Longarm muttered as he took the stairs as fast as he could manage.

At the top of the steps he found chaos. Nearly every room door except his own was standing open. Hotel guests stood in the open doorways staring toward the end of the hall where the floor's bathroom was located. The clerk, the bell boy and a heavyset man wearing a badge and a large revolver were at the far end of the hall.

Jimmy was inside the last room. So were two corpses and what looked to be several gallons of blood that was fresh enough to be still spreading on the floor. The dead pair looked like their heads had been run through a meat grinder. On each of them the damage—and it was considerable—was confined to the upper torso and head.

Jimmy the Kid had his shotgun cocked and leveled in the general direction of the local lawman. The bandages that concealed whatever the expression on his face was gave him the look of a madman, something out of a nightmare.

"Ease off, Jimmy." Longarm said as soon as he reached the doorway and got a look at the mess inside.

"They didn't give me a choice, Longarm," Jimmy said in a rush. "I came down to use the crapper. The man . . . that one over there . . . he saw me. He knew who I was. I guess he didn't see that I had the gun. It was hanging on this side here and my other side was closest to him. He pulled a gun on me. Told me to get in this room here. The woman was here. She picked up a gun too. That little one lying over there on the floor. It was on the bureau. They . . . I don't know for sure what they intended to do, but I know it wouldn't have been good.

"The man . . . I don't know his name but I've seen the drawings of both Bradley and Bob Dekins and it wasn't either of them . . . the man looked at the woman. He told her to shoot me. He said the noise from her little pistol wouldn't be as loud as from his .45.

"That's when I brought my gun up and . . . and shot them, Longarm. I had no choice. I really didn't. I'm sorry. But I promise you, I had no choice. They were both armed

162

and they intended to shoot me." Jimmy sounded a little scared and certainly he was nervous. Longarm wondered if he'd had time to reload the shotgun. Probably. Longarm had taught him to do that before he did anything else, just in case he needed more than the two shots.

From the looks of things here two shots had been more than enough.

"You aimed for the heads," Longarm said.

"Yes, I did," Jimmy said, his tone of voice suggesting he damn well had and would do it again if need be.

"Good shooting," Longarm told him.

"Who the hell are you?" the local lawman sputtered, "And is this man really a United States marshal like he claims to be?"

"Yes sir, he sure is, an' so am I," Longarm said. He pulled out his wallet and flipped it open to display his badge.

"You don't look like marshals," the lawman grumbled. "Not neither one of you."

"We did until we walked into a bomb up in Arnpelt a while back," Longarm told him.

"That was you? I heard something about that."

"That was us all right. An' the bomb was planted by that woman over there."

The lawdog's eyes went wide. "That pretty thing?"

"You knew her then?"

The man nodded. "She was real friendly. Came to me, oh, a couple days ago. She wanted to know if the streets were safe for a lady here in the wild west." He frowned. "Come to think of it, she wanted to know how many deputies I have . . . which ain't none, I have to do all the lawing that's done here . . . and, well, things like that."

"Which you told her," Longarm said.

"Of course I did. I wanted the little lady to be comfortable here. This is a quiet town. Did I hear your, uh, partner there say your name is Longarm?"

"It's what I'm called. My proper name if you want it is Custis Long. That fellow over there is Deputy United States Marshal James Wheelock. An' Jimmy, I think you can point that gun o' yours down now. An' maybe let the hammers down."

"Oh. Right."

The local man looked toward Jimmy and shuddered. Apparently he hadn't realized how very close to death he could have been. "My . . ." he coughed, "my name is George Waters. I'm the town constable."

"It's a pleasure t' meet you, George."

"I heard about you, Longarm. I, uh, if you say this man was engaged in the line of duty, well. . . ."

"*He* says he fired in the line o' duty, George. An' his word is plenty good enough for me."

"Yes, well . . . uh . . ."

"We'll get out of your way now, George." Longarm motioned for Jimmy to join him.

"What about, uh . . ." Waters gestured toward the two bodies.

"Whatever you want t' do with 'em," Longarm said. "Hell, might could be there's reward money out on the man." He paused and reached for a cigar, deciding to treat himself to a panatela instead of an ordinary cheroot. Then he grinned. "Might be a little hard t' figure out who the man was though. Ain't much face left on him to go by."

George Waters looked like he might very well puke. Not that it would have mattered much. The hotel room was already so messy that a little vomit would hardly be noticed. "I suppose the town will have to bury them," he mused.

"Look on the bright side, George. They might have a

good bit of cash on them. The town can use that to bury 'em."

"And to pay for cleaning this room?" the hotel clerk put in, speaking for the first time.

"Talk t' George about that. He's in charge here now."

That seemed to please the constable. Until he took another look to see just what it was Longarm said he was in charge of. "Jesus," he groaned.

"Yeah," Longarm agreed, motioning Jimmy toward the room. Jimmy leaned close and whispered, "I'll be with you in a minute, Longarm. I came down here to take a crap and I still have to go. Bad."

"Fine. Then come back to the room. An' Jimmy . . ."

"Yes?"

"This time try an' do what I tell you, okay?"

"Yes, I . . . I'm sorry. You told me to stay in the room. I know. But I had to go so bad. And I hate to use those damned crocks. You know?"

"I know, but this time it's cost us a chance to interrogate those two so we could find out the gang's plans. Go on now. I'll be in the room waitin' on you."

"Yes. Sorry." Jimmy turned away.

"All you spectators can go back inside your rooms now," Longarm said loudly as he made his way down the hall again, "unless you want t' come look at the blood. Anybody wants t' see a woman with her head blowed off, come take your look 'cause now's your chance."

Of the five people staring into the corridor, only two went back into their own rooms. The other three actually took Longarm's facetious suggestion at face value and hurried to the end of the hall so they could stare open-mouthed and bug-eyed at the carnage inside the dead woman's blood-splattered room.

Good Lord, Longarm thought. *People!*

Sometimes he just couldn't understand them.

And Jimmy the Kid, damn him, was going to have to do some explaining when he was done shitting, never mind what Longarm had said to the constable about Jimmy's yarn being good enough on its surface. Longarm just naturally had to wonder what the kid hadn't said about the shooting.

Chapter 34

"All right, goddammit, did you at least have sense enough to get some information out of that pair before you executed them?" Longarm was burning hot and his voice and expression showed it.

"I didn't . . . I already told you what happened," Jimmy protested.

"Bullshit! You told that town clown a nice fairy tale, and you're lucky. He believed it. I ain't so gullible, Jimmy. I saw where your buckshot landed. An' I know a thing or two about the spread that comes outa that short little barrel o' yours. Remember, kid, I been with you all this time when you was practicing with the thing.

"I know you weren't firing from across the damn room when you took those two down. If you was, the shot spread woulda put pellets in them at least down to waist level. But that ain't what happened. Your shot was concentrated nice an' tight and aimed at their faces.

"That was deliberate, Jimmy. Those shells was fired at close range. Real close. They couldn't of been more than four, five feet away from you. Maybe closer.

"And that, Jim, tells me that the yarn you spun for Constable Waters . . . an' for me, I might add . . . was just so much bullshit.

"Now what's done is done. I can't change it, and I ain't gonna turn you in to the Attorney General. I would except you've said yourself that with one eye and only one hand you aren't gonna be carrying a badge after we get back to Denver an' report in to Bill Vail. So there's no use in me charging you with anything. Hell, a former deputy marshal with your handicaps wouldn't live out the first week in any prison I've ever heard of. I won't do that to you, Jim. But I won't accept any more bullshit from you either.

"Now tell me what happened in that room. An' tell it to me straight." Longarm was more than a little pissed off. He made no effort to hide that fact.

Jimmy hesitated at first. Then, defeated and quite probably more than a little ashamed, he sat down. Longarm could not see because of the bandages but the huskiness in Jimmy's voice when he spoke suggested that the kid was crying now.

"I . . . you're right. It didn't happen the way I said."

Longarm waited for Jimmy to work up the nerve that would allow him to continue.

"I saw . . . I was watching. When that girl came upstairs after breakfast I peeked out. I saw what room she went into. I wend down there to have it out with her. I was in the hallway when the guy came upstairs. I didn't want anybody to see me go into her room. I guess . . . I guess I thought I could . . . could punish her for what she did to me, for ruining my life. I guess I was thinking I could do it and nobody would know it was me if no one saw me go inside that room. So I went into the bathroom.

"I heard the guy come down the hall and knock on her door. I heard her open it and invite him in. The son of a

168

bitch's name, by the way, was Charley. I didn't hear a last name, but she knew him. He was part of the gang.

"She didn't lock the door after she let him in, so I just . . . just walked in on the two of them. I covered them with the shotgun and backed them up against the bureau."

Longarm grunted. He sat on the side of the bed and folded his arms, waiting for Jimmy to finish his story.

"I confronted them. Demanded to know what the gang was planning. They said . . . they said they wouldn't tell me."

"The gold," Longarm said, "will arrive by rail on the 7:15 westbound this evening. I intended for us to cover it from a distance since no one here knew anything about there being any U.S. deputies in town. Now that plan is blown all to hell an' gone thanks to you. We'll have to do it some other way now."

Jimmy nodded. "I'm sorry."

"Are you?"

Jimmy's chin came up and he squared his shoulders. "I am sorry that I ruined your plan about taking the gang by surprise. Don't expect me to be sorry that Charley and the girl are dead."

At least that sounded honest enough, Longarm thought. "All right. Go on. Tell me the rest of it. What did you find out from them?"

"I gave Charley a chance. I let the hammers down on my gun and I told him to draw on me if he thought he was fast enough. I guess . . . I think that convinced him that I wasn't playing around with them. I wanted an excuse to kill them. Instead of going for his gun he took it out nice and careful with just two fingers and laid it on the floor.

"I cocked my shotgun again and aimed it at the woman's face. I reminded her that she was the bitch who blew my face off. I showed her what was left of my hand

169

and said I was going to take these bandages off so she could see what was left of my face.

"She started to cry then. I think perhaps she knew I was going to kill her. I told her that her only chance was to tell me everything she knew. She believed me."

Longarm just grunted. And waited for Jimmy the Kid to continue.

"In addition to Charley there are five gang members at the moment. Brad and Bob, of course, and three others. She called them Bobby, Clint and Pecos. They're all five waiting outside of town. Charley came in to see if the girl . . . her name was Patsy, by the way . . . to see if she'd spotted any marshals here or a large army presence to help guard the shipment.

"She said the gold is supposed to be guarded on the train by some Pinkertons, but they are working for the railroad and are there to make sure the railroad isn't liable in case of theft. There is supposed to be a paymaster in charge and two enlisted men to help carry the chest. Between here and Fort Larned there will be just those three soldiers."

"There won't be a detail sent out from Larned?" Longarm asked.

"There was supposed to be, but the wire giving the order for a wagon and escort was intercepted by a collaborator. A soldier. He is the one who tipped the gang to the whole thing. He's doing it in exchange for half of the gold."

"Shit," Longarm said. "Half? That'd be the day."

Jimmy nodded. "Charley and the girl admitted that the soldier would be killed when he came to collect his fee for setting the job up."

"How much gold is there supposed to be?"

"More than twenty thousand dollars is what they told me."

"That's the same thing Billy's wire said. He says it'll be twenty two thousand for the Kiowas plus whatever payroll is owed to the caretakers at Fort Larned. Did they tell you the name of the turncoat?"

"No, I don't think either of them knew it."

"Did they say anything about the effect this would have on the Kiowa? It would start a war, damn them. People would die all over the southwest if the Kiowa break out and go back to the warpath."

"They didn't say anything about that," Jimmy responded. "I doubt that they would have cared as long as they had their share of the loot."

"Bastards," Longarm muttered. After a moment he fixed Jimmy with a cold stare. "They spilled their guts to you, Jimmy. So why'd you shoot?"

"It was . . . that was the reason I went down to that room, Longarm. I went there with the intention to kill that woman for what she did to me. And you were right about me being close to them. I wanted to get a good look at her. I wanted her to get a good look at me.

"I heard them out, Longarm, and then I shot Charley in the face."

"Just like that, Jimmy?"

"Yes. Just like that."

"And the woman?"

"She was terrified. She dropped down to her knees. She begged me not to kill her. She offered her body to me. She said I could have her any way I wanted. She said she would go with me and I could use her for as long as I liked."

"Were you tempted?"

"Not even a little bit," Jimmy said in a dead cold voice. "If I could have I would have let her suck me off before I killed her, but I knew people would be coming to the sound of that first shot. So I didn't have time to savor the pleasure. I just," he shrugged, "I just shot her. In the face. I did to her face the same thing she did to mine."

"Yeah, well, it's done now. An' I reckon I need your help to take the Dekins boys down. I'll tell you something though, Jimmy. Soon as we have those sons o' bitches in custody, I'll be wanting your guns. Your badge too. Thinking of you bein' a deputy marshal makes my skin crawl."

"The bitch deserved to die," Jimmy said.

"That's for a judge an' jury to decide, kid. Not us. It ain't never up to us."

Jimmy stood and went to stare out the window with his back to Longarm.

Fuck him, Longarm thought.

He wondered if there was time enough to go out to Larned and get the men there to come help guard that gold. Probably not, dammit. And anyway he did not know which of the soldiers out there was the turncoat who intercepted that telegram. And who was stupid enough to think the gang would give him a fifty percent cut as a finder's fee.

No it was up to him to handle this. And, damn it, he would need Jimmy Wheelock to do it.

Damn it all, though. Just . . . damn it!

Chapter 35

It was not quite dark when Longarm and Jimmy the Kid finished their supper at a café near the depot and made their way to the platform.

"Don't you think they will see us here?" Jimmy asked.

"Sure, they will. But there's no sense tryin' t' hide. They know we're here. They'll be looking for us."

"But Charley never reported back to them. How would they know?"

Longarm said, "By now they will 've got fretful about their man going missing on a simple trip to that hotel t' see the girl. They will 've sent somebody else in to ask around, and in a town this size you can be damn sure the shooting this morning will 've been the big news of the day. The saloon talk will 've been about little else." Longarm looked at the kid and scowled. "You really fucked us up, Jim."

"I won't apologize. I had the right."

"Bull. But we'll talk about that again later if you like. Right now I need your help. You an' that shotgun you're so proud of."

"I didn't . . ."

"I don't wanta hear it, Jimmy. Now hush your mouth an' take up a spot over there by that baggage cart. They know we're here anyway. Maybe we can scare them off by showing ourselves. It ain't likely, but right now the important thing is *not* the Dekins gang. Get that through your head Jim. Right now the important thing is t' get this reparation money to those Kiowa headmen so there won't be another Indian war that people fight and die in. We can worry about the Dekinses after the gold is safe where it belongs."

"Why are we coming all the way down to the end of the platform then? Shouldn't we be up by the ticket office? That's where the freight will be brought."

"We're down here because I figure the gold—An' the soldiers, an' the Pinkertons—they'll likely be in the mail car. The engineer will stop with the passenger cars beside the platform. The mail car will be somewhere down in this area when they come to a stop. I wanta be as close to it as possible. Now be quiet, like I told you. I've had about a bellyful of you, Jimmy."

"I'm sorry."

"About executing that woman?"

"No, but I am sorry that I've made you mad."

"Jesus!" Longarm shook his head. "Just . . . be quiet, will you please?"

Longarm pulled a baggage cart around to a position he liked and sat down on it so he could lay his crutches aside. If the gang tried to take the gold here at the station, Longarm wanted both hands free.

Following Jimmy the Kid's example with his shotgun, Longarm had rigged a temporary sling on his Winchester. He tied a leather thong around the lever and carried the carbine slung over his shoulder. The arrangement was awkward when he moved, the dangling carbine bumped and banged against his crutch, but at least it al-

174

lowed him to carry the weapon and use the crutches at the same time.

Longarm settled down and pulled the bulbous old railroad quality Ingersol watch out of his vest pocket. It was only 6:04. The westbound train carrying the gold was due at 7:15. The Dekins boys would not be happy if they intended to take the gold at the platform.

Longarm placed the Winchester across his lap and sat calmly, his right hand draped comfortably on the carbine's grip. He could not claim this was a good arrangement, but under the circumstances with both him and Jimmy pretty thoroughly crippled there just was not very much else they could do except make a show of defense and hoped it worked long enough to protect that reparation money and avert a war with the Kiowa.

"The train is late," Jimmy said at a quarter past seven.

"It'll be here." Longarm said it with confidence but he had a sudden, gut-wrenching thought that the Dekinses could have been spooked away from town by the deaths of Charley and—he'd said her name was Patsy? yeah, Patsy—the brothers could have altered their plan and decided to wreck the train somewhere east of town, then loot the wreckage. And kill whoever was still alive. Jeez, they could have decided to do it that way. And there would be even more deaths as a result. Soldiers, Pinkertons, train crew and passengers. The Dekins brothers wouldn't give a shit. Longarm damn sure would. He felt a tremendous surge of relief when he heard a train whistle in the distance.

The westbound clanked and hissed its way to a halt at 7:28. Close enough. A porter hurried to set steps down for the passengers. Closer to where Longarm and Jimmy waited, the door to the mail car was unlocked and pulled open by a man wearing a suit and carrying a Winchester.

An army major and two privates stood in the doorway looking around.

"They won't be here," Longarm called to them.

"What? Who won't be where?"

"The guard detail from Larned that you're expecting. They won't be coming."

"They are supposed to be here," the major protested.

"Yeah, but they ain't gonna be." Longarm picked up one of his crutches and waved it so the major could see. "I'd come t' you but that's a little difficult for me right now. I'm a U.S. deputy marshal outa Denver, and I reckon you and me better have a talk before you pull that chest off the train and lose your Pinkerton protection."

"You aren't supposed to know . . ."

"No, but I do an' so do some other people that really shouldn't. So if you don't mind, sir, I'd appreciate it if you'd come over here so you and me can have a talk."

"All right. But my men and these other gentlemen will be keeping an eye on you."

"Fine." Longarm pulled out his wallet so he could display the badge and satisfy an obviously skeptical army paymaster.

The major climbed down from the mail car while his soldiers and the Pinkertons stood by with their rifles ready.

Once Longarm satisfied the officer as to his identity he motioned for the man to take a seat beside him on the baggage cart.

It took a good ten minutes for him to explain the situation—and the danger—to the paymaster.

The officer's response was a heartfelt, "Oh, shit!"

Chapter 36

While the train conductor bitched and moaned about his schedule, Longarm and Major Tremaine held the westbound—and the Pinkertons—where they were until Tremaine could go wake the livery man and hire a farm wagon.

The rig was a heavy old son of a bitch with a deep box made of thick oaken boards and pulled by a pair of huge draft horses. It was, Longarm thought, perfect for the job.

It was past 8:30 and full dark by the time Tremaine had the wagon in position and the gold could be transferred from the mail car to the wagon bed.

"You boys 'd be welcome to join us," Longarm told the Pinkertons once the chest had been placed in the wagon along with a satchel containing bronze medallions that Tremaine intended to present to the Kiowa leaders as gifts from the Great Father.

"I wish we could, Long, but we have our orders. We have to stay with the train."

"I understand. Thanks for your patience with us."

The Pinkerton glanced toward the engine where the

conductor and engineer were fuming and sending evil glares toward Longarm and the soldiers. The man grinned. "Not so patient maybe, but at least it's done. Reckon we'll go now."

The Pink waved toward the conductor. The train was already in motion before he could get back to the mail car. He had to jump to make it inside before the train picked up speed.

"Now we'll hope they haven't been watching what we been doing here," Longarm said. "With luck they oughta be waiting for you somewhere along the road an' not know about our little surprise."

"If it is a surprise," Tremaine said.

Jimmy helped Longarm into the back of the wagon, then climbed in himself. The major and one of the soldiers got in too and the other private closed the tailgate and latched it, then went around to get on the driving box and take up the lines.

Longarm and Jimmy sat on the floor, weapons in hand. The sides of the wagon box were more than high enough to hide them from view. Major Tremaine sat on the gold chest, which lifted him high enough that the top of his head could probably be seen from outside the wagon. The other guard stood behind his friend on the driver's seat.

The soldiers both had Springfield rifles, single shot weapons in .45-70 caliber. The cartridge carried a wicked punch but was slow to fire. Major Tremaine had a .45 revolver.

Even with the firepower Longarm and Jimmy the Kid could offer, Longarm would have liked to have more. But then if he were wishing he might as well ask for a troop of cavalry to ride along with them too.

The hell with it, he thought. You do with what you have, not with what you want. He sat with the Winchester in his lap and endured the pounding of an unsprung wagon on a rough road.

"Jesus?"

Longarm heard the dull thump of a bullet striking flesh, the yelp of the guard on the driver's seat and the bark of a gunshot at almost the same instant.

They seemed to have found Bradley, Bob and friends.

The wagon lurched sideways and the guard who had been driving jumped for the protection of the thick side walls of the wagon box.

"Sons o' bitches killed the off horse," the soldier reported while his companion returned fire with a round from his Springfield. The muzzle flash was unpleasantly bright in the darkness of the night.

Longarm grunted. He'd been more or less expecting that. Shooting a horse was the most effective method of stopping any sort of wagon. The occupants might as well be nailed in place because in order to move again someone would have to leave the wagon and cut the dead animal out of the harness.

There was a flurry of gunfire from both sides of the road, and the other horse went down as well.

"I guess they don't intend t' use this wagon to carry the gold away," Longarm said. "Remember what we said now. Just go easy an' hopefully none of us will be the ones getting' hurt."

Tremaine and both of his men crouched low in the wagon. There was more gunfire outside and the rattle of bullets striking hard wood, but the oak sides were thick. None of the slugs penetrated.

"Don't shoot any more," the major shouted. "You've already wounded one of my people. There's lead and splinters flying everywhere. Stop shooting. Please."

"You surrender?"

"Yes. Yes, I do, damn you. Just stop the shooting before we're all killed."

"Throw down your weapons," a voice came back from the darkness.

"You can't expect . . ."

"The hell we can't. Now throw them out or we'll riddle that wagon and everything in it. You prob'ly wouldn't like that. Us now, we wouldn't give a damn. So we're leaving it up to you. Throw out your weapons or we go back to shooting."

"All right. All right."

Tremaine nodded, and the two soldiers briefly stood and threw their awkward, slow firing Springfields onto the road. The rifles landed with a clatter.

The men ducked down again and Longarm could hear footsteps close by.

"It's all right, Brad. They tossed the rifles all right. I got them here," a voice called.

"All right then. You soldierboys, you all stand where we can see you."

"Easy now," Longarm whispered. "We'll wait for your signal. Tell us which way they're coming."

"To the back of the wagon. They're headed for the tailgate," Tremaine said in a barely audible voice.

Longarm and Jimmy rose to a crouch, Jimmy's shotgun and Longarm's Winchester at the ready. Longarm was forced to hold his splinted right leg out at an angle and take all his weight on his left leg. The position was not comfortable but he had no choice about it.

The soldiers, men and officer alike, moved to the front of the wagon box. Tremaine was holding his revolver down by his side, cocked and ready. He would be responsible for anyone approaching the front of the wagon. His men, unarmed now, would be responsible only for getting the hell out of the way when the shit began to flow.

Longarm could hear movement on the ground outside. The robbers were close. He could hear footsteps beyond the tailgate.

"Now!" Tremaine barked.

His soldiers dropped to the floor.

Longarm and Jimmy jumped up.

"What the . . . !"

Jimmy's shotgun roared, spraying the road with buckshot, while Longarm snapped off three, four, five shots from his Winchester, then palmed his .44 and turned it loose as well.

He dropped one robber with his first shot, missed another with the rifle while the fellow dropped down and rolled frantically in the dirt to escape Longarm's bullets.

The Colt accounted for another of the gang while the remaining robbers turned night into day with continued muzzle flashes.

Longarm could hardly see, his night vision destroyed by the sheets of flame from muzzles both inside the wagon and out.

He could see well enough to return fire wherever he saw one of the robbers shoot. He heard screams.

Jimmy reloaded, the sound of his breech snapping shut distinctive even in the midst of the fight, then the scattergun bellowed again. One barrel and quickly the next.

Longarm emptied his Colt and shoved it back into his holster, taking up the Winchester again.

But there were no more muzzle flashes coming from outside the wagon now.

Longarm became aware of Major Tremaine standing at the tailgate with a smoking revolver.

"Are they all down?" Longarm asked.

"I think so. I know I got one of them at the front. By the time I got back here it was all over, I think."

"Jimmy?" Longarm asked. "How'd you do with that shotgun?"

There was no answer. Jimmy was still standing. The white linen bandages on his head made him stand out in the darkness.

Jimmy turned very slowly to face Longarm. His shotgun fell onto the floor with a sound that seemed unnaturally loud in the silence that had followed the continuous roar of gunfire.

"No . . . apologies," Jimmy said in a low voice.

Then he collapsed on top of his shotgun.

"Damn!"

Longarm hopped on one leg to the other side of the wagon. Tremaine reached Jimmy the Kid first and knelt to feel for a pulse. When he stood again he shook his head.

"I'm sorry, marshal," the paymaster said.

"Don't be. I think the kid was hoping this'd happen. I think in a way he was looking forward to it."

Tremaine sighed. Then straightened and began giving orders. His men needed to find the horses the gang had been riding. They had to be somewhere close by. Then they would need to muscle the dead draft animals out of harness and put the gang's ponies in their place.

"Will you come with us, Long?" he asked.

"Reckon I don't have much of a choice. I can't ride and sure as hell can't walk back to get my buggy. Which come to think of it I'm gonna leave right where it is. I'll take a train t' get back to Denver."

"Will you help us determine who the traitor is in the caretaking detail?"

"That, I am glad t' say, is an army problem. I done what I needed to about the Dekins boys. Your gold is safe an' the

Kiowa will be going home happy. I expect that's about as far as I can take it, major. We'll let you an' likely a board of inquiry work out the rest of it."

"As you wish, sir."

Longarm sighed and took a seat on top of the chest that held the reparation money. He looked at James Simpson Wheelock III lying crumpled and bloody on the floor of the stout old wagon.

"Shit," he said. And turned his attention elsewhere.

Watch for

LONGARM AND THE UNGRATEFUL GUN

the 327ᵗʰ novel in the exciting LONGARM series
from Jove

Coming in February!

**Explore the exciting Old West with one
of the men who made it wild!**

JAKE LOGAN
TODAY'S HOTTEST ACTION WESTERN!

J. R. ROBERTS

THE GUNSMITH